MW01129140

M&K Tracking
by Kate Danley

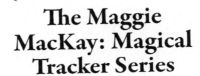

The Maggie MacKay: Magical Tracker Series

http://www.maggiemackaymagicaltracker.com

DEDICATION

To New Beginnings

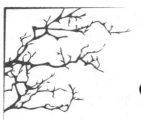

Chapter 1

M&*K Tracking*. I admired the newly re-lettered door featuring our company name in glorious gold letters. It was close enough to the old business my dad and I ran, *MacKay & MacKay Tracking*, that hopefully return customers wouldn't get too confused. I wanted to glom onto whatever street cred we MacKays had, because I was sick of our current spate of scraping the bottom of the barrel nonsense. Ever since Dad left the family business, folks seem to have decided they wanted to let someone else figure out whether his snot-nosed kid had the chops to take over. Let's just ignore the fact that I was running this place by myself for three years while Dad got himself trapped in an inter-dimensional prison. They'd see. But if things didn't change, I'd have to start running coupons for *Buy One Staking, Get the Second FREE!* I would just leave out the part that after our recent experience with the vampire race, I'd happily throw it in gratis. Shoot, I'd pay *them* for a good excuse to start poking things with sharp objects.

It would sure eat the pants off of what I had going right now. I opened the door to our office and walked inside.

My name is Maggie MacKay. I'm a magical tracker, able to open dimensions and walk between the worlds of Earth and the Other Side whenever someone or something has overstayed its welcome. Killian is my new partner, a six-foot-something forest elf whose favorite dumb party trick is using his wood-ish ways to charm the pants off of anything with two legs. At least I think two legs is where he draws the line.

Killian and I had been having a go at this business part-nershipiness for about a month now, opening up shop after we saved the world... again... and my dad's decision that being trapped in an inter-dimensional boundary between worlds, freeing a town full of ghosts, and bringing his daughter back from a time-vortex was enough adventure for any man's career.

So Killian stepped up to the plate, making the excuse that he should be around in case the werepire Vaclav decided to show his ugly mug. Killian also made some noise about the MacKay Tracking killer health benefits — 'killer benefits' is a tier in Other Side Omniversal Healthcare for those who spent a lot of time battling things out with bad guys. No co-pay.

But we all knew the truth: the lure of tromping through the forest to talk to bunny rabbits didn't hold the same appeal it once did for Killian. Slaying vampires will do that to a per-son. He wouldn't admit it, but I knew Killian was looking for an excuse to hang out in the presence of my awesomeness and dust some vampire fangs. And even grumpy ol' me had to ad-mit Killian had proven his worth. Plus, tall people are nice to have around when you need to reach things on top shelves.

So, here we were, one full moon-cycle into running our very own agency. It was in the same one-room affair my dad and I had occupied, sans evil landlord. Yes, most landlords are evil, but this one was eviler than most, and I'm not talking about rent hikes and deferred maintenance. Mr. Smith turned out to be a vampire bent on our destruction. He died under mysterious circumstances which I know absolutely nothing about. Nothing.

But since he died, no one had shown up to collect the rent. Inheritance rights are a little fuzzy on the Other Side. Personally, I think he probably ate his next-of-kin long ago. But these things usually come down to a winner-takes-all-unless-a-lawyer-gets-involved situation. Since no lawyers had shown up and no one seemed to notice and/or care that Mr. Smith was dead, I went ahead and filed the paperwork down at City Hall. Once we finished paying the back taxes, the building would officially be ours, and as soon as *that* happened *and* our luck turned around, we were going to remodel this place into the next Taj Mahal. Okay, so maybe the inner guest-room closet of the Taj Mahal. But shwanky enough to be Taj Mahal adjacent, nonetheless. You know, *if* we could get some business going. I tried to tell myself it was just a seasonal slump and maybe evil had taken a holiday, but you know things are bad when you keep hoping *someone* would show up to make your life a living hell.

Speaking of slumping and making my life hell, Killian was hunched down in his chair, legs propped up on his desk, reading this week's briefs on the back of his eyelids. Slacker.

"Killian! We got a gig!" I announced as I dropped the stack of folders in his lap.

He startled awake, practically falling out of his chair as he tried to explain, "I was—"

I looked at him, daring him to even try. "—sleeping on the job?"

He smiled and rubbed his face with his hand. His elfin blues twinkled up at me. "Contemplating the meaning of the universe. Really, Maggie, where is your benefit of the doubt?"

I was suddenly awash with warm feelings, a winter's day before the fire, snuggled close to a loved one. The whole world looked like I was viewing it through a gauzy haze of romance and candlelight.

Fucking elf.

I smacked him with a file folder upside the back of his beautiful, blonde head. He winked and turned off his glamour, allowing the room to return to the usual state of menace one expects living and working on the Other Side.

I flung myself into my wooden chair and started unpacking my pockets. "Up late partying?"

"Solstice," he admitted, resting his forehead in his palms.

"That's still two weeks away..." I said as I dumped my gun into my drawer.

"You know how the elfin people can be with their holiday celebrations..."

"Sad that it's become so commercial," I replied. You could barely walk into a shop without being inundated with decorations and cards, not to mention the non-stop carols. If I had to listen to one more radio station play *It's the Most Wonderful Light of the Year*, some disc jockey was going to be seeing permanent darkness.

"Well, nothing shakes off an ambrosia hangover like a little work," I chirped.

"You are a terrible liar."

"It's why you love me."

Killian picked up the files I dropped in his lap and put them on his table. He held his head carefully as he flipped through. "Please tell me it is not another gargoyle outbreak."

I guiltily went over to the stack, took the top five cases, and shuffled them to the bottom.

He looked at me. "Truly? More gargoyles?"

I shrugged my shoulders.

One gargoyle. We happened to befriend just *one* gargoyle named George on a haunted cruise ship and Frank, the one-eyed ogre at the Other Side's Bureau of Records got wind of it and fast-tracked us into winged garden gnome retrieval - a.k.a. gargoyle round-up. Good old, Frank. Always looking out for us.

It's not that gargoyles are tough to bring in, they're just tough to take down... from the eaves of a cathedral. They spend their nights gallivanting about the roof peaks of various religious centers like a pack of heathen monkeys. With the light of day, they freeze into those fun little stone-carved statues that so many goth kids are in lurve with.

Wasting your time and energy trying to capture them while they are running around is an easy way to get oneself killed. They have a reputation for being able to scare-off evil, and that's because they are scarier than evil. It's a fight-fire-with-bigger-fire fight, which is sometimes just what the doctor ordered. More times than not, though, it is a whole Pandora's Box of awfulness when you use gargoyles to handle a pest control problem.

So more days than not recently, Killian and I would find ourselves stuck rigging climbing harnesses and ladders and belay lines and then marching off to the far distant corners of some crumbling roofline to chisel away the unwanted gargoyles where they sat. Yes, chisel. With a chisel. Gargoyles like to bind themselves to roofs. Want to know what they use? Poop. Gargoyle poop. They poop and then sit in it and then it all turns to stone and it is a pain in the ass, pardon the pun, to un-cement them from their perch. And, mind you, you have to start off at the crack of dawn to get it all done before sundown because you do not want a reanimated gargoyle in your car. Trust me on this one. Trust my car upholstery and my busted trunk.

So it is up at sunrise, find where the gargoyle moved to in the middle of the night, climb up, chisel him off, don't think about the petrified garg-poop, transport a frickin' rock statue down to the ground without dropping or breaking him, cross back to the Other Side, and turn in the slab. Then race home to rinse off of all the gargoyle dust because when the moonlight hits you, it has a nasty little habit of transforming into a stinky layer of gargoyle crap.

Like I said, gargoyles are bigger than evil.

And there were a ton of these cases.

All coming our way.

And Frank was loving it.

"Can you inform Frank we are not available for gargoyle removal anymore?" Killian begged.

I walked back to my desk. "I, unlike you, you tree-dwelling elf, have a thing called a 'mortgage' that needs paying and, evidently, this is all Frank's got going on right now."

Killian sighed. "I suppose we should consider ourselves fortunate for the opportunity." He picked up the next folder.

"I wonder why the sudden outbreak in gargoyles," I mused as I settled into my chair again.

"Perhaps they're breeding."

I leaned back in my seat. "Fantastic. The gargoyles head over to earth for a little R&R and are humping in all our high holy places."

"It is a perfectly natural biological..."

"Yeah, but it takes all night for them to get hard."

"Maggie..."

"When did joining the Mile Heavenly Club become all the rage?" I said, spinning in my chair.

"You can cease."

I stopped and shot finger-guns at Killian. "I guess if one of them calls out 'Oh god' they're actually close enough to hear the answer."

"You realize if we are struck by lightning, this will all be your doing."

"Gives the phrase 'Holy fuck!' a whole new meaning."

"Are you done yet?"

I sighed. "Yes."

"Shall we go?" he asked.

I hauled myself to my feet. "Yep."

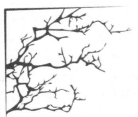

Chapter 2

"A little more to the left," I shouted helpfully.

The gargoyle had tucked himself tightly into a little eave of Father Killarney's church there in the heart of Hollywood. Chiseling him out was gonna be fun. For Killian.

He was clinging to a ladder as our retrieval bucket swayed softly in the breeze, slightly below our criminal statuary. He was sporting a pink bike helmet Mindy leant us and some knee pads. Someday we would be able to afford a cherry picker and this whole process was going to get a helluva lot easier. You can't carry a boulder down a ladder, so ropes and buckets were where we were at. Killian started scraping and I held the ladder tight. Like I said, we had a partnership. Now, you might be asking yourself how he got to be the lucky bastard up on the top rung while I was stuck far below. Well, evolutionary speaking, elves are better climbers than humans. Okay, so not really, but I figured if Killian was dumb enough to fall for the statistic, I was smart enough to dish it out.

"You're doing great!" I shouted at him.

Father Killarney wandered out, shielding his eyes with his hands. "Looks like we have a little yellow bird up on our windowsill."

I re-established my hold on the bucket rope. "Just cleaning out some vermin for you, Father."

We were lucky that we didn't seem too out of place. Ever since the epic battle with the horde of dopplegangers on Father Killarney's front steps, he had been raising funds to do some repair... erm... 'restoration work' on the 'historic property'. There was scaffolding around the far side of the building and construction equipment everywhere.

"You could leave him if you like," he said as the sound of Killian's chisel filled the air. "I've always been appreciative for the gargoyles looking out for us."

"Wish I could, but he was supposed to just be here on vacation," I replied. "Frank would have my head. Plus, the entire tracking society would have a great big laugh that Maggie McKay couldn't even bring back a gargoyle in broad daylight."

"No chance of extending his stay with a work permit?"

I shook my head. "Sorry, Father. It's the bureaucrazy. Once that gargoyle broke the rules, he got himself a one-way ticket."

Father Killarney sighed, "A shame. I suppose you'll need to take the rest of them, then."

I looked at Father Killarney sharply. "Rest... of... them...?"

He started to say something and then stopped himself. "I should show you."

From the look on his face, this thing he wanted to show me was not a storage room filled with gargoyles pre-packaged in rolling suitcases ready for an easy trip to the Other Side.

"Killian?" I shouted.

"Yes?"

I could tell by the tone of voice now was not a good time.

"How close are you to being done?"

Killian grunted and I heard the sound of stone sliding on stone. "Almost... got... him..."

The weight on the rope took a dangerous dip as the gargoyle fell out of Killian's arms into the bucket.

"Bring him down, Maggie."

I slowly let the rope out of the winch. Killian put his two feet on either side of the ladder and slid the whole way to the ground. He made it in time to catch the bucket before its arrival. I ran and opened the door to my car. He carried over his living boulder and dumped it in the back seat with an "oof!"

He wiped the sweat from his brow with the back of his hand and removed his pink helmet. One shake of his head was all he needed to fluff out his boyish curls like he was the star of his very own Pantene commercial. "Now. You were in need of something?"

I jerked my thumb at Father Killarney.

Killian looked at me warily. "Please tell me he does not have another one..."

Father Killarney waved at us to follow him, guilt written all over his Irish mug. We walked around the church to the school's cement playground. Foursquare courts and worn-out basketball hoops littered the yard. Father Killarney kept walking, passing through the chain link fence to the parking area. Along the alley was a row of white stucco garages with white wooden doors.

Father pulled a key ring out from his belt. He looked like he could have been a jailer.

"Now, don't judge me. Leave that for God," he said, fitting his key into a padlock.

The priest was making me nervous. "Don't make me turn into his avenging angel, Father. Show me what you gotta show me."

Father Killarney pulled up the garage door.

I groaned.

Lining the garage, like chickens perched in a hen house, were rows of gargoyles.

"Father Killarney... What were you thinking?" I asked.

Father Killarney rubbed his hands nervously. "Now, before you go saying anything, they came to me for sanctuary."

"That's what all my skips say."

"You might not believe me, but I have an obligation to protect all of God's creatures."

"You couldn't have picked puppy dogs?"

"The gargoyles said that they are fearful of a great outbreak of evil. They're looking out for me as much as I am looking out for them."

"I hardly think..."

"You *should* think, Maggie. Think about what it might mean when I've got a garage full of gargoyles who feel the need to come protect my church," he said, his voice getting high pitched as he waved his arms around like I was missing something important. "Gargoyles don't. just. show. up," he said slowly.

I looked at their sleeping, roosted forms. This was a nightmare. No way could Killian and I remove a single one of them without breaking one of their toes. And what if Father Killarney wasn't talking crazy and they actually were here for a reason? I looked at Killian and he looked at me. I rubbed my face with my hand. "FINE! You win." I could hear Killian exhale a huge breath of relief. I elbowed him to get his shit together. We were professionals now and I needed to at least pretend like Father Killarney was walking on thin ice. I pointed my finger at the priest. "I didn't see anything, but only because you're a friend of the family. You tell those gargoyles of yours if any of their paperwork comes across my desk, there is nothing I can do. Tell them to keep their files current. I'll try to get them a work permit to be out here, okay? But don't push me."

Father Killarney patted my shoulder. "Thank you, Maggie-girl. Just one last thing..."

"Yes?"

"Would you two please find out what evil force is being unleashed and causing them to come here?"

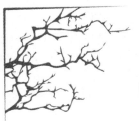

Chapter 3

Killian had been relatively silent the whole ride from Father Killarney's church on Earth to the prison intake where we needed to dump our skip on the Other Side.

I flipped off the radio. "Care to fill your partner in on what those wheels in your head are churning?"

He looked at me, as if suddenly remember that he was in a car with me and a stone gargoyle, who, may I point out, was looking at me between the seats with his petrified angry eyes every time I glanced into the rear view mirror.

"I was contemplating what might have caused the gargoyle influx..." he replied, shifting in his seat.

"Yeah..." I sighed. "If they had some sort of organized leader, we could ask him. But, unfortunately, they are too terrifying to hold city council meetings."

Killian shook his head. "Maggie, have you ever heard of that many gargoyles appearing in one place before? Legal or otherwise?"

"Um... Notre Dame?"

"What?"

"In France."

I could see Killian scroll through the textbooks in his mind. "Yes. I remember... The cathedral in Paris with the hunchback. What was his name?"

"The hunchback... of Notre... Dame...?" I offered.

Killian rolled his eyes at me, a sign we were spending way too much time in one another's company. "No. His proper name."

"OH! Quasimodo. Heard of him?"

"Rings a bell."

"Ha ha." I groaned. And then saw that Killian wasn't even aware of what he had done. "Heard he opened up a shop on the Other Side after all that nastiness with the pitchforks and the fire."

"He is still alive?"

"Think so. I mean, osteoporosis hit him a hundred years ago, but you can't really tell."

"So this Notre Dame Cathedral has gargoyles?"

"Yep, gargoyles and a bunch of other permanent guards. Union gig. Heck of a retirement plan."

"What is their duty?"

"Guarding relics. The place was gutted by a vampire mob during the French Revolution. The gargoyles hang out to make sure it doesn't happen again."

"But these are not union gargoyles. They are voluntarily breaking Other Side law to gather. Are there any threats of mobs attacking Father Killarney's church?" asked Killian.

"I can't think of anything he's got of any value..." My voice trailed off. "I mean, other than himself..." I thought back to how he was kind of instrumental in taking down my Uncle Ulrich and cleaning up the desecrated churches that Vaclav was hoping to use as portals to the Other Side. "The vampires wouldn't hold a grudge against him, would they?"

Killian laughed. "Vampires? Holding a grudge? Why, you are mad to suggest such a thing."

"Shit."

Killian patted my hand. "Think on the positive side. It is most likely just vampires. It could be worse."

"I don't think that is thinking positively, Killian."

I pulled up in front of the Other Side police station and yanked on my parking brake. "Wait here. I'll be just a minute."

I popped open the door and picked up the gargoyle. I swear he weighed 2.3 million tons. He was as uncooperative as a cat in a harness. I lugged him inside and rolled him onto the reception counter. I rang the little bell to let them know I had arrived.

"You did not just put a gargoyle on my counter," said Lacy as she came out of the office kitchen.

Lacy is a blue woman in charge of intake at the Other Side prison. If Pamela Anderson licked Willie Wonka's wallpaper without blowing up into a blueberry, you'd have Lacy.

"Order up! Hot and ready, delivered in thirty minutes or less," I said, dinging the bell again.

She pressed a button on her phone and spoke into the intercom. "I am going to need a cart at reception. Cart at reception, please."

She pulled out her intake book and started pushing the papers over to me to sign. "Do you have any idea how hard it is going to be to sweep up all that dust before the moon comes up?"

"You're preaching to the choir. My partner is covered in it."

"You're making me long for the days that you showed up on my doorstep with a baggie of ghoul goo."

"Tell Frank to start sending us after less foul prey."

"You better believe I'll be making that call." She leaned over and pressed the intercom button again. "I said I need a cart at reception. Does anyone even work around here anymore?"

I heard the shuffling feet of the zombie porters. You'd think hiring zombies would be an unwise move, but zombies are after brains and there is little risk in a government facility.

"Finally! Get this gargoyle outta my sight, please," Lacy barked.

I watched as the zombies slowly rolled the gargoyle onto their cart and rolled him away. By the time they were gone, Lacy had finished cutting me my check.

She held it out with two fingers and gave me a wicked little smile. "So how is business going over there at M&K Tracking?"

"Booming," I replied dryly as I took her money.

"If that partner of yours ever needs a personal assistant, you make sure to pass along my number," she said, giving me a wink and a hitch of her hips.

Lacy was hot to trot after Killian. As was the rest of the world. Elves and their frickin' glamour.

"Trust me. You're on his short list," I said.

"Oh, I've got a long list of things I could do for him. Glad to see you kept him around."

"I needed someone to carry my gun."

"I'd be happy to carry HIS gun."

"I'll pass that on!" I said, heading for the door. "Gotta go!"

Lacy shouted after me, "Next time, you send that partner of yours in for the check, ya hear?"

I plopped down into the driver's seat and started up the car.

"Everything proceed accordingly?" Killian asked.

"Your girlfriend sends her regards," I replied, holding the check up with two hands and making it dance.

Killian smiled. "I look forward to the day when our business is in need of reception services."

"If you snag Lacy using magic, it's cheating," I informed him as I revved the engine.

"Cheating, you say? Breaking the rules? Do you think she might punish me?"

I flicked the tip of his pointy ear. "Watch it, elf."

We meandered through the streets of downtown Other Side until we arrived at the entrance of the Elfin Forest. The forest is surrounded by a low brick wall with a black iron fence on top. The wall fronts the visitors' entrance to their land. The gate is made of cast iron and looks a lot like Central Park. It's the sort of spot that looks like an invitation for some punk kid to hop over. The Elfin Forest, however, is not Central Park and you don't go for a stroll in there as a non-elf if you want to live. Seriously, you do not mess with the elves. They will take you out. We're not talking violence. We're talking they will look into your eyes and, channeling the voice of Mother Nature, tell you that they are deeply, deeply disappointed. Then they will hammer it home with a little reverse glamour of guilt. THEN they'll take you into the middle of their forest and let you try to find your way out. And that's just for the idiots who trespass. If you've got something wicked in your mind, they'll just shoot you on the spot and let you bleed, all while your mind replays your biggest regrets en loop before you die. Elves. They get in your fucking head.

And that is why, other than that one time I saved Killian by transporting us in, I had never actually been inside the elfin forest. And why I never offered door-to-door service when I was giving Killian a ride home. And why he never invited me in to see his pad.

I pulled the car to a halt and reached across to open Killian's door for him, anxious to get him out so I could get cleaned up. "See you tomorrow."

He unbuckled his seatbelt. "Do you have any amusements scheduled for the evening?"

"Vacuuming up gargoyle dust. Then burning the vacuum."

Killian reached out his arm to give me a hug and I shrunk back. "Not until you wash that dirt off you."

He laughed and leaned over, giving me a peck on the forehead. "You know you enjoy it dirty."

Killian jumped out of the car, closed the door, and gave himself one quick shake. The gargoyle dust flew off his body and onto the ground in one easy poof. He took off into the forest at a loping jog and for the first time ever, I wished I was an elf. For hygiene purposes. Only.

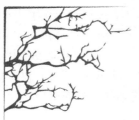

Chapter 4

I dropped my car off at a carwash that was just a couple blocks from my house. They had a weeping llorona whose tears could wash away anything. My car would definitely give her something to cry about.

I opened the front door to my house and flipped on the lights. I owned an arts-and-crafts style cottage which a real estate witch pulled right out of my head and custom grew for me. The wooden floors matched the honey-colored beams in the ceiling which matched all the cabinets in the place. I couldn't wait to plop my big, fluffy butt onto my big, fluffy couch and knock back a beer as I watched *Spelling with the Stars*. Nothing gave my night a boost like seeing some pretty boy try to figure out what to do with eye of newt.

Mac, my fat orange tabby, came rushing to the door to greet me. I gave his head a little rub after he bonked it against my leg. I rifled absentmindedly through the mail and breathed a great big sigh of relief that there was nothing but junk mail and local ads for sales on Solstice curses. Ah, nothing brings out the best in people quite like the holiday spirit...

I sat down at my desk and pulled out our ledger to track this latest take. I deducted the cost of the car wash, what we owed on back taxes for the property, and sighed looking at all the little numbers in all their little columns. Somehow it seemed like they should add up to something bigger. I had no idea how my dad did it. Business expenses plus the expenses of keeping a family of four watered and fed... shoot. Disappearing into the boundary was sounding better and better. I was going to have a tough time keeping just myself watered and fed.

My cell phone rang and I picked it up.

"Maggie! You're coming over for dinner tomorrow night, right? I'm picking up the ingredients for the lasagna and want to make sure you're coming so you can bring home leftovers."

I looked at my clock. "Hey, Mom. Can't talk too long. Need to go rinse off some gargoyle dust before sunset, but yes, I'll be there."

She started to say something, but her voice crackled and popped out as the signal died. Wireless service on the Other Side is not exactly what you would call "good". Too much magic in the ether and gremlins in the cell towers. The phone rang again.

"Hey, Mom!"

There was stillness on the phone, but I could hear the dude breathing. It sounded like nails on glass.

"Hello?" I asked.

There was no answer.

"If this is a telemarketer, you better hang up now. I am on the 'Do Not Call Because I'll Come Through The Phone And Rip Out Your Still Beating Heart' list."

"Maggie MacKay?" hissed the voice on the other end.

"Finally! You speak. Yes. What can I do for you?"

"Do not accept the job that comes in tomorrow or we will kill your sister."

You know how you can tell a Chihuahua from a Saint Bernard without looking at them? This guy might have been barking in English, but there was nothing human about him. There was a scratching rasp to his voice and that rasp told me I most likely had myself a vampire on the line. Also, the death threat. I breathed deep. "You realize that by threatening my sister, you just made me automatically decide to take the job, right?"

I could hear the guy get really confused and murmur to someone else in the room. He got back on the line. "Well, how do you know we were not trying to manipulate you? We wanted you to take the job, so we threatened your sister, so if you want to thwart us, you must not take it."

Some guy in the background whispered, "That's good! That's good!"

Great. Not just vampires but idiot vampires. "Listen, jack-holes, I'm a hired gun. I take whatever job pays the most. You want me to not take a job tomorrow? Bring a bucket full of money to my office and give me a million reasons not to take it."

"That is all it would take?" hissed the dude on the line.

"NO, you jerks. You went and threatened my family," I shouted, "which means this is now personal and I wouldn't take your money if you showed up on my doorstep with three million buckets filled with gold coins."

"We could arrange that."

I gulped. "Are you a leprechaun?"

The thing laughed, "No. But our master knows someone who is."

I rolled my eyes. Everyone says they know a leprechaun. It's one of the oldest pickup lines in the Other Side. "Well then why don't you tell your 'leprechaun' to take those buckets of three million gold coins and shove them up the end of your rainbow."

I hung up.

The phone rang again.

"WHAT?!" I shouted into the receiver.

"Maggie!"

"Oh, sorry Mom," I cringed. "Sorry..."

"I tried calling back but I kept getting your voicemail."

"Sorry, there was just a thing with work that came through."

I am a horrible liar, especially when it comes to lying to a psychic. I waited for her to call my bluff. Fortunately, it seemed like my fib was close enough to the truth that it didn't set off any of her bells and whistles.

"Well, you just tell them to contact you during normal business hours. How in the world did they get your number? *And* think it was appropriate to contact you home? Really. These clients of yours, Maggie." I could hear her banging around the kitchen, opening and closing cupboard doors. "Although you're never in your office to receive their messages even if they did try to call. I can't tell you the number of times I've tried to reach you there and the phone just rings and rings and rings. Perhaps it is time to invest in a good receptionist."

I wondered if Lacy and Killian had been talking to her. I rubbed my eye as I opened up the refrigerator, looking for something to dull this out. "Don't worry. Killian is already on her... this... Killian is already on this."

"Well, good. I'm glad someone there has good business sense."

"We only have two employees, Mom."

"Like I said."

I wondered if I could convince those vampires to pass on my sister and take me instead. I reached for a six-pack in the back of the fridge. "Hey Mom? Is Mindy coming tomorrow night?"

"No," she replied. "She has a big work event. Why?"

I popped the cap on the longneck. "Oh, just thinking I might have a funny story to tell her."

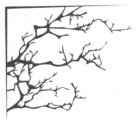

Chapter 5

I sat at my desk cleaning my gun as Killian fiddled around. He was busy hanging plants from the ceiling and draping vegetation all over the windows.

I watched him suspiciously.

"What?" he asked, turning away from his stringing and pounding.

"You have quite the eye for office improvements," I remarked, staring at the green profusion. His side of the office looked like a goddamned forest.

"You do not see its appeal."

"No. It's great. I love... things... like plants... living... everywhere..."

"You are a terrible liar, Maggie."

"I am a fantastic liar," I replied.

He motioned to his handiwork. "I am merely enhancing our security systems," he explained.

"Killian. Vampires avoid the morning, not your damn Morning Glory."

"This office has so little life in it, the undead would feel quite comfortable," he informed me.

I looked at all the greenery. It was definitely alive. I envisioned how quickly a little spell could cause one of the vines to come over and choke us, but tried not to think too much about it. Just because it happened with one man-eating plant doesn't mean it is going to happen again, but still...

"Just keep it over on your side," I growled at him as I re-assembled the pistol and cycled the action.

Killian shook his head. "Living things that you care for and nurture are not harmful to you, Maggie."

"I would beg to differ," I replied, giving my gun one last wipe.

The phone rang. Killian and I both made a dash for it. I beat him.

"I win," I mouthed.

To the victor come the spoils. Killian gave me a dirty look as he grabbed my coffee cup and crossed the room to refill it.

"MacKay and... M&K Tracking," I answered.

"Maggie! Honey! How is business?" my mom chirped.

I looked at Killian. "We haven't killed each other yet."

"It is only 9AM."

"We're doing even better than I thought."

"Honey, I have a job for you."

"What do you need me to pick up at the grocery store?" I asked, grabbing my pad and pen.

"No dear, I have a job for you."

I sat forward in my seat. This seemed odd. "Dad can't give you a hand with this?"

"He says he won't let me drag him back into this sort of thing. Swears he's retired. As if you get a choice if you're retired. I see that look in his eyes and know he really wants to, but will he? No. He just needs to admit this is a lifelong vocation—"

"What can I help you with, Mom?" I interrupted.

"Maggie, you remember Mrs. Hamilton?"

Mrs. Hamilton was a friend of my mom's. "Yeah..." I said, knowing where this was going.

"I need you to run over to her house and pick up a package for me."

Crap. I looked at the receiver. "Really? I'm being reduced to errand girl?"

"Well, I know that you're looking for jobs and I thought this might be a nice one that doesn't involve gargoyles."

"MOM! I don't need your pity jobs."

Killian whispered, "Yes, we do."

I waved him away.

So, here's the deal with the Other Side: the entire place is infused with magic. It is, quite literally, seeping out of its pores. And spores. If you want to enjoy just a regular cup of tea, you have to get it from Earth. The stuff grown on the Other Side will have you peering into the future and communing with past ancestors. You wouldn't believe the cost for a regular bag of Lipton's.

So, while I would be more inclined to just hit any old grocery store closest to the portal, my mom had a tea lady she's been buying from for years: Mrs. Hamilton. They actually went to school together back in the day, marching in the marches, and fighting the good fights. And now, Mom and Mrs. Hamilton do an even exchange. Mom gets her regular loose-leaf tea. This lady gets her magical leaves. It is a win-win all the way around. Except for me, who, apparently, was being nominated as Most Likely to Shuttle Their Nonsense Back and Forth.

"Maggie, honey, I need these items anyways and it was either pay $50 for shipping from Earth to the Other Side or pay you $50 for shipping."

"Can I pay $50 to have someone else do this?" I groaned.

"You are being ridiculous. Do you have something better to do today?"

I looked over at my stack of stupid cases. Those statues weren't going anywhere. I mean, they were, but I was pretty sure I could figure out where they ended up tomorrow morning.

"I'd be happy to go pick up a package at Mrs. Hamilton's house," I sighed, pulling out my pen and pad. "What's her address again?"

Killian's eyes lit up and he was as giddy as if I had just announced we were throwing a surprise party for a five-year old. I got the details from Mom and hung up.

"Well?" he asked.

I pushed myself back from the desk. "Quick run to Los Angeles. Quick run back."

Killian rubbed his hands gleefully.

"Don't be so happy," I grumbled.

"Will this involve any stabbing?" he asked.

"No," I replied darkly.

"Punching?"

"No."

"Shooting?"

"No."

"Gargoyle poop?"

"No." I sat back in my chair and groaned at the ceiling. "It is THE WORST."

He shook his head. "Maggie, I believe your priorities and mine might not be in alignment."

I sighed as I got up and grabbed my coat. "You know, I got a call from a vampire last night telling me not to take any jobs today. I should have listened to the bastard."

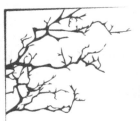

Chapter 6

I walked up the uneven sidewalk towards the little 1940s bungalow in Alhambra. The neighborhood was teetering on the edge as the original homeowners died off and the folks moving in didn't seem to see the point in mowing grass. I shoved my keys in my pocket as Killian brought up the rear. Most likely to get a good look at my rear.

"Stop looking at my butt, Killian."

"Merely protecting your back," he replied.

"My backside can take care of itself," I informed him.

"It does appear that a great deal of care has been taken towards it."

I was contemplating the benefits of changing M&K Tracking to a sole proprietorship when Killian flung his arm around my shoulder. "See? It is impossible to be angry about this job if you are angry at me."

I glowered at him. "I've always been excellent at multi-tasking my rage, Killian."

He put me in a headlock and kissed the top of my forehead. "It is not as bad as you think."

"I can't believe my mom is getting me into the shipping business," I said, glumly. If any of the other World Walkers get wind that I have becoming nothing but a glorified courier service...

"It is better than the smuggling business."

"Marginally."

"Do you recall how we almost died with the Combs of the Empress? And the Jade Lion?"

"Those were good times, Killian," I replied.

"You are sick, Maggie."

I opened up the metal latch on the chain link fence and walked up the concrete walk to the little blue house with its little white awnings. I knocked on the white metal door and a woman came to answer the rattle. She had beautiful skin, darker than coal, and her short, natural hair had gone steel-gray. She wore a rock wrapped up in some copper metal, which hung from a thong around her neck. Her clothes were knit and loose, painted with some sort of water-colored picture of indistinguishable something. She beamed as she recognized me. "Maggie! You here for the tea? Your mom said you might be stopping by!"

"Yes, ma'am," I replied, shifting uncomfortably as I noticed her notice Killian.

"So, is this your new 'friend', Maggie?" Mrs. Hamilton asked, like she was ready to help my mom start booking wedding caterers.

"No, Mrs. Hamilton, this is my partner."

Yes, I called her Mrs. Hamilton. I could be ninety-years old and with one foot in the grave, and I would still call her Mrs. Hamilton. That woman never had to raise her voice over a whisper, and she'd still have every kid in the neighborhood apologizing to her for their bad manners. She was just one of those people.

She leaned against the doorframe and looked him up and down. "Is that what they call it these days? I never can keep up."

"I mean my business partner," I clarified, to make sure she understood the situation here. "He's taken over since Dad retired."

"Mmm... how lovely to have such a fine-looking young man helping you keep shop," she commented.

Killian nodded sagely, agreeing with her wisdom.

"He's neither as young nor as helpful as he might look," I replied.

"Mmmhmmm," she said. "Aren't we all?" Mrs. Hamilton handed me the paper bag and I gave her the one from Mom. Hers was a lot larger and heavier than mine. She must've seen the look on my face because she explained, "I was cleaning out my pantry and found a meditation bowl that your mom always said she liked. After she mentioned how things are going with your dad in retirement, I thought she might appreciate it. Someday when you and your partner set up housekeeping, I'm sure you'll appreciate the joys of quiet meditation."

She gave Killian a knowing wink.

"Thank you, Mrs. Hamilton!" I said, ready to be done with this. "Great to see you, ma'am! Killian and I need to go! Ma'am!"

She had me all flustered.

"A pleasure to make your acquaintance!" Killian called as we walked away, waving at her over his shoulder. I could hear her knowing chuckle following us down the sidewalk. Killian turned to me. "She seems like a very nice person."

"She is," I replied.

"Not grumpy at all."

"Nope."

"Perhaps you should consider meditation, Maggie."

In that moment, while I was trying to decide where to punch him, I failed to keep an eye on our surroundings. A dark shadow jumped out of nowhere and grabbed Mom's bag of goodies. Not some sort of shadowy figure. It was, literally, a shadow.

"Awwwww shit," I said. "He did not just grab that from my hand."

I took off down the street with Killian close behind.

"And here you thought you were having a bad day!" Killian yelled.

I laughed. "Things are looking up!"

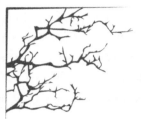

Chapter 7

"You go that way! I'll go this way! We'll cut him off at the corner!" I yelled.

Killian split and took off like frickin' Carl Lewis. I swear, if Other Siders are ever allowed to enter in the Olympics, the rest of the world can kiss their gold medals goodbye. Running for your life almost every night tends to weed out the less fleet of foot. Evolution is a bitch.

I tore off down the other side of the block and tried to distract the shadow. There weren't a whole lot of trees or shrubs for him to hide in. It was street cleaning day and most of the cars were gone, too. Just large, expansive swaths of weedy lawns. At the end of the long block, there were some rundown convenience stores and old Laundromats. I was hoping to get the shadow before he got that far and could hide himself inside of an industrial dumpster.

"Hey! Get back here!" I shouted, hoping that maybe if it was looking at me, it wouldn't pay attention to the pointy-eared blur coming fast from the other direction.

The shadow looked back and tried to double his speed.

Now, this is the thing about fighting shadows. They're shadows. If you're on the Other Side, you don't want to chase them into a dimly-lit alley, because they'll join up with all their buddies in there and drag you into the Dark Dimension. On

Earth, though, they're operating at around 10% power. There aren't any portals directly to the Dark Dimension, so between having to do a jump through the Other Side to get to Earth and the lack of magic once they arrive, shadows usually can't do much besides hang out in the corner of your eye and spook you at night.

The other thing about fighting shadows is that they are two-dimensional. They have to either fall on the wall or the ground, always at an angle to the sun ('suns' if you are on the Other Side). Yes, they can hide in pools of darkness, but this one was carrying a bag of tea leaves and a clanking metal bowl, so it was pretty easy to spot. It almost looked like someone had tied a string around the bag and was dragging it around like some sort of practical joke.

The joke was on the shadow though. Like a lot of things with roots in the Dark Dimension, it doesn't like the taste of silver, and I was packing more sterling than a flatware sale at Neiman's. If you can thwack them hard enough, you can pin them like a cockroach in a bug collection.

And my silver throwing-star seemed to do the trick.

The shadow was stuck to a telephone pole, his scrawny arms flailing.

Killian FINALLY turned the corner and saw that I had already bagged the guy. Or, seeing how I was now the one holding the paper sack, de-bagged the guy.

"Now, most folks would have been happy to see you, Mr. Shadow, but I ain't Peter Pan." I swung the bag between my two fingers. "This is called theft. But since I'm carrying weapons, I'm going to call it armed robbery."

I took my other throwing star and pinned him right through his two-dimensional dingleberries.

Killian winced.

"You want to tell me why you are hanging around Earth robbing demure little ladies like myself?"

The shadow shook his head.

"Dollars to donuts, you want something in this bag, is that right?" I pulled out my lighter. "And I'm just betting you're here on Earth without a permit."

He began shaking his head, as if he was trying to explain something.

"Listen, shadow. It's nothing personal. Caught you fair and square, right?"

The shade looked defeated.

"Killian, you wanna get a bottle for me?" I asked.

He patted his tights, like magically he was going to sprout a wallet. Killian has sprouted many things out of his pants, but a wallet has never been one of them. "I am afraid I do not have any of your Earth money," he said.

"I've got some cash," I replied, not taking my eyes off the shadow.

Killian came over, reached into my back pocket and grabbed five bucks.

"Watch how long your hand is on my ass there, elf."

"Merely retrieving funds, Maggie," he said, giving my bottom a comforting little pat.

I rolled my eyes. "Elves, you know?"

The shadow shrugged his shoulders in agreement.

The main street to the neighborhood was just a couple blocks away and we waited as Killian wandered down to the corner store and then came back, sipping a bottle of water. He still wasn't done when he got back to us. I started to speak, but he held up his finger politely as he continued to drink. You'd think after however many centuries he'd been around, Killian would've picked up how to shotgun a beverage. The elf never would have made it through a frat hazing. I put "introduce the elf to a beer bong" on my mental to-do list. After another century of sipping, Killian was done. He turned towards me ready for instructions.

"Okay, Killian, I'm going to keep him pinned and you get to catch him," I explained.

Killian's eyes sparkled and he confessed to the shade. "It is my first catch. This is very exciting."

I held the lighter towards the shade in warning. A lighter doesn't do permanent damage to a shadow, you would need a spotlight to obliterate them, but burning them through the belly-button isn't a pleasant experience. This one seemed like he was ready to play nice.

Killian opened up the bottle. "By the power invested in me by the authority of the Other Side, get in the bottle."

I withdrew one star, then the other, and didn't even have to click my lighter. The shade went inside and Killian put on the lid. It looked like someone had bottled up some ink.

"Good job, Killian!"

He gazed at it like a kid with a jar full of fireflies. "Look! He is right in there!"

I patted his shoulder. "You're absolutely right."

"And the best part?" he said proudly. "It is not a gargoyle."

"Indeed, it's not a gargoyle."

We walked back towards the car, Killian grinning from ear-to-ear. "What a splendid day, Maggie!"

"See what I'm saying? This is SO much more fun."

"And we did not even come close to death."

I opened up the backdoor to my car and put the bag on the seat. "Well, maybe if we're lucky we can do that tomorrow." I covered it up with a blanket, just in case someone else was looking for it. "Wonder what was so important that something from the Dark Dimension would head over to pick it up..."

"Can I drop off the shadow with Lacy?" asked Killian. "Perhaps she will reward me..."

So much for childlike joy and innocence. "Sure, Killian."

I revved the car.

Chapter 8

"Hey Mom! I brought your tea! Left it in the tea room!" I said as I walked through the kitchen and planted a kiss on her cheek.

Mom was busy at the stove, humming to herself. She was dressed in her blue, house frau muumuu, featuring small calico flowers. Her hair had been freshly permed and formed around her head like an orange poodle.

"Oh good!" she said. "I'll grab it in a second."

She'd been a whole lot happier since Dad quit almost getting killed every night. Can't say I was sorry for the shift in mood.

My parent's place was a shotgun style townhouse. The front was the psychic eye shop where Mom had been reading the leaves of any paying customer since the family moved here almost twenty years ago. Psychic eye shops on the Other Side were about as exotic as Starbucks on Earth, but Mom also served up the tastier, non-mystical tea for special clients and that gave her a leg up in this world.

It was separated from the rest of the house by a beaded curtain. Walk through and you'd find yourself in the kitchen, the dining room, and finally the living room. Pop out the backdoor and there was a small yard with a detached garage on the far end. The family part of the house was decorated in sort of early-

American 1950s colonial décor. Lots of golds and browns and dark, cannonball furniture left over from when Mom and Dad first got married.

I wandered into the living room, passing Dad as he set the table. The Other Side evening news was playing loudly enough from the walnut-encased TV that Mom could hear it in the kitchen. Same old monsters and mayhem, mixed in with a couple of feel good Solstice stories. There were aluminum trays stacked up next to the television, but from the looks of things, tonight we were eating in the dining room. My parents had a sturdy, but banged up, table with a permanently sticky finish from thirty-years of spilled drinks. There was a matching hutch, which I always thought would have been more at home in the captain's quarters of a tall ship than our digs. It was filled with the old, chipped china that had survived my sister and me growing up. Every now and again, Mom would mumble something about redecorating, but she never seemed to get around to it.

Dad came behind me with his arms full of tableware and handed the stack of plates over. "Guess what you have to do before we let you eat?" he asked.

"No such thing as a free dinner, huh?" I said.

"Nope. Get to work."

Dad was enjoying his semi-retired state. His shaggy, dirty-blonde-and-gray hair was growing out even more and he looked like maybe he was getting regular naps. He spent his days puttering around the firing range and trying to keep Mom's appointment calendar in line. It was kind of silly, since she could sense when someone was coming or not, but it was sweet.

As I set a plate on the table, I yelled, "Oh! And Mrs. Hamilton sent a meditation bowl, too. She said you might want it."

"Oh how lovely!" Mom shouted back. "That was very nice of her."

I heard the beaded curtain rustle and then Mom brought the bag into the room to talk to us as she unwrapped it. She pulled the meditation bowl out and set it on the table. "Well, wasn't that nice of her! I always loved this old thing."

"So what's so special about it?" I asked.

"It has a lovely tone," she replied giving it a tap.

It was like listening to ice crack across the pond. I slammed my hand down on it to make it stop ringing.

Mom looked at me like I was crazy. "You know, meditation could do you good, Maggie."

I looked over at Dad. He was as pale as I felt.

"Did you feel that?" I asked.

He nodded.

Mom looked at us quizzically. "What is it?"

I picked up the bowl. "The tone of this bowl just shattered the boundary like an opera singer with a wine glass."

"What?" she asked.

I pinged it again, this time a little harder. The boundary fissured like I had just thrown a stone at a tempered window. I watched, holding my breath, hoping that the boundary would not collapse completely. "This is definitely not helping me clear my mind."

Chapter 9

Dad and I had been sitting there for a good ten minutes playing with that bowl. We'd tap it and watch the dining room air fracture like a spider web and then heal up again.

Mom was not nearly as amused. "Are you two done yet? Dinner is going to be ruined."

I shushed her with my hand as I hit the bowl again. "What do you think, Dad?"

He leaned back in his chair. "I've never seen anything like it. How long did Mrs. Hamilton have this?"

Mom put her hand on her hip and leaned against the chair in exasperation. "Oh, since she was a teenager at least. We used to use it in school to calm our nerves. Now, can I pull the lasagna out of the oven so we can eat dinner?"

"So the perfect tone," I said, barely hearing her, "which, magnified by the resonance of people's thoughts..."

"That would do it," said Dad.

He gave it a good hard whack. It crazed the boundary all the way from the living room to the kitchen. It never entirely broke through the boundary, just messed around with it.

"So it just weakens the boundary," I observed as I reached out to see how hard it would be to push through.

Dad stopped my hand. "There's nothing through the boundary of our house for six dimensions you want to go playing with, Maggie-girl."

Some people build a moat around their castle. My dad liked to pick homes in the middle of dimensional abysses.

Mom threw up her hands and went into the kitchen.

"Even taking into account the fact it is easier to make portals here on the Other Side," Dad pointed out as he turned the bowl over again, as if this time someone's signature would magically show up on the bottom, "if you have just a modicum of talent, you could use this to open illegal portals wherever you wanted to on Earth."

"I should keep it in my glove compartment. Make it easier to get home."

Dad shook his head and jerked it towards where Mom disappeared with a look of 'you are an idiot for saying that in front of your mother'.

"No, the responsible thing would be to destroy it," he replied, shaking his head to indicate there would be no destroying going on.

"I wonder how many of these are being used for that very purpose?"

Dad gave it another ting and we watched it crack the air again.

"I got a weird call from a vampire last night," I said absentmindedly.

"Maggie! What have we told you about talking to vampires!" Mom shouted from the other room.

"It's okay! It's okay. I thought I was picking up the phone to talk to you." I hit the bowl again. "He said if I took the job today, they were going to kill Mindy. I wonder if this is what they meant."

Mom walked calmly out of the kitchen to the phone in the living room. She dialed with one finger and looked back at me, shooting daggers from her eyes.

"What?" I said.

"Mindy? Honey? You're alive and everything is all right?... No, I didn't feel anything. Your sister just mentioned that a vampire might want to kill you."

I heard Mindy shouting in the background.

"It is okay, honey. Your house is warded. Your dad and I are coming to stay with you since your sister has to hunt the bastard down."

There was even more shouting in the background. Dad got up and started unpacking luggage from the coat closet.

"Don't you make me feel bad about this!" I yelled at him.

"You shouldn't have taken the job, Maggie," he said.

Mom put her hand over the phone to back him up. "You shouldn't have taken the job!"

"You were the one who hired me, Mom!"

"That is beside the point. You don't see your sister taking jobs that get you killed."

"She is an accountant!"

"Numbers can kill!"

"No, they can't!"

"Don't argue with me, Maggie! I am very upset right now." She ducked back into the kitchen, trailing the long spiral cord behind her.

"Why? Do you sense something?" I asked.

"You are perfectly aware that I can't read my own fortune!"

"You're reading Mindy's fortune," I pointed out.

"Don't argue semantics with me!" she said, banging around dishes.

"Listen, the vampire was dumb as a box of rocks. Nothing is going to happen," I groaned as I walked into the living room and flung myself in one of Mom's brown velour armchairs.

Dad came back and patted my shoulder. "It will be fine. We'll just go over for a little while to make sure things are quiet at Mindy's. Keep your phone on, Maggie-girl. And don't go getting yourself into any trouble you can't get out of."

"I've got Killian on speed-dial with bail money."

"Of all people, *Killian* should have known better. I mean, I would have expected this from you, but from *him?* He should have forced you not to take this job," Mom chided, coming into the room with the phone on her shoulder. I could still hear Mindy yelling on the other end.

"He was just really excited to be involved with something that didn't involve gargoyles," I explained.

"If he didn't want to deal with gargoyles, he should have become a plumber," she said, shaking her finger at me.

"That doesn't even make sense."

"Why are you getting so many gargoyle cases?" Dad asked. "We never had that many."

"I don't know," I groaned, so not wanting to go into this.

"Did you upset Frank?"

"No."

"Did you?" he asked again, this time more sternly.

Jeez. "Yes," I admitted, but then added so that he could see it wasn't my fault. "But no more than usual. And I'm not the reason there's been an outbreak of rogue gargoyles around Father Killarney's church."

"Is something trying to come through?" he asked, not letting up.

I leaned back and counted the ceiling tiles. "A shadow tried to steal the bowl from us this afternoon."

"Wait... a shadow from the Dark Dimension?"

"DID YOU SAY YOU FOUGHT A SHADOW FROM THE DARK DIMENSION!?" Mom yelled.

"NO!" I shouted back. "It was just a shadow."

"It was from the Dark Dimension, wasn't it, though?" asked my dad.

I looked at them both guiltily and then nodded.

"And they were after this bowl?" he asked, picking it up like it was Evidence A in some sort of bad episode of Perry Mason.

I could see where he was going with this. "Yep."

"A bowl which creates portals?"

"Yep."

"A creature from the Dark Dimension was after an object which creates portals?" he spelled out very slowly for me.

I sat back in my chair and wiped my face. "Yep."

He shook his head and stood up. "Okay, we'll bring the bowl with us to Mindy's."

I groaned. I knew one guy in two worlds who was an expert in portal-creating objects. If anyone knew anything about anything, I was going to have to pay a visit to Chinatown. I held out my hand. "No, stop. I did this. I'll take care of it."

Dad put his arm around Mom. "Hang up the phone, dear."

Mom turned back to the receiver. "We'll be there in an hour, Mindy."

The smoke alarms started going off.

"Oh no! That's dinner!" she shouted and ran for the door to clear out the smoke.

There went my leftovers.

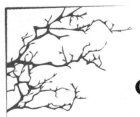

Chapter 10

I always knew I was in for it when I got off the freeway at Hill Street and the first Asian inspired buildings came into view. I was like Pavlov's dog, only instead of salivating, I was suppressing the urge to throw up all over Chinatown. Give me a vampire or werewolf over Xiaoming any day. The man was a grump. Although, I guess when you need to have something put away for a rainy day, you gotta pick the guy so grumpy no one is going to mess with him. Shoot, *I* wouldn't mess with Xiaoming if I didn't have to.

I parked my car and headed towards his orange-painted metal gate. The dusty steps led to his apartment and I had to take a big deep breath to steel my courage before I walked up.

The two concrete lions were sitting right there. The moment I came onto the landing, those fuckers both turned their heads and looked at me. I held up my hands in peace. "I just need a moment of Xiaoming's time."

They weren't having any of it, though. They slowly lifted themselves up from their pedestals and came to their feet.

"Xiaoming!" I shouted.

Both lions' mouths broke out into a growl.

"XIAOMING!" I shouted louder. His lions looked like they were just about to pounce. I wracked my brain trying to remember how you are supposed to fight animated concrete.

"What is it? You so loud." The old Chinese man shuffled towards the door and opened it up. Same ratty robe. Same falling-apart terry cloth slippers. Same stains on the same striped boxers. He looked at his lions in disappointment. "I told you I was not to be disturbed. Why you letting her in?"

They settled down onto their pedestals.

He shook his head. "Concrete lions not work so good since they have that fight with your werewolves."

"What are you talking about? I'm feeling lucky they didn't eat me," I replied.

He waved at me dismissively with his hands. "They not eat you. They just grind your bones to dust. What is your problem? You worry too much."

Personally, I felt that was something worthy of being worried about.

"I'll be out of your hair in a minute," I promised.

"You bringing more werewolves here with you?" he asked, pointing his finger at me accusingly.

"No. No werewolves or vampires or anything, Xiaoming. I just need you to look at something and tell me what it is. Then I'll leave and hopefully we won't have to see each other for a very, very long time."

He took a long drag from his cigarette and dropped the ash on the carpet before giving me a grudging nod of his head to follow behind.

I walked into his house. I don't think he had changed a darn thing since I first came with Killian. Okay, I guess he changed a couple things because his living room had been torn apart by werewolves looking for us a few months ago. But the way he had put it all back together again looked remarkably like how it was before.

"Did you use magic to clean up?" I asked.

He shrugged his shoulders. "It not magic. I just remembered them. Many things get sad when they are forgotten. I just make sure my sofa know it is remembered and it gets better for me. No one likes to be lonely."

"Are you lonely, Xiaoming?" I asked.

He looked at me like he was going to reconsider feeding me to his concrete lions. "What you want?"

I pulled the bowl out and showed it to him.

"What? It is a bowl. You put some noodles in it and you eat some dinner and you go home."

I rolled my eyes. "Yeah? Well can your table setting do this?" I hit it with my fingernail. The boundary cracked a little and the concrete lions gave a growl to let me know they did not approve of whatever it was I was goofing around with. "Wanna eat noodles out of it now, Xiaoming?"

His face got all tender and sweet. He was looking at that bowl the way I've seen some parents look at their baby's first step. The guy might have even teared up.

"What?" I asked, completely mystified why he would be having this sort of a reaction.

"This is the bowl of a very young apprentice," he replied. "We all have to create bowl like this when learning how to craft magical objects."

"Wait. You're saying to me there are other things like this out there?" I clarified.

"Of course," he said, looking at me like I was an idiot, which is not much different than how he usually looked at me. "You think this is the only piece of magic in the world, Maggie MacKay? You think only you able to make portals?"

"Well, I had been led to believe that what I did wasn't exactly common."

He clucked his tongue and shook his head. "You think you special snowflake. You not snowflake."

"My mom thinks so."

"You even have twin. You even less than snowflake."

"No, I'm just more special because there are two special snowflakes who are exactly like one another. We're a matched pair. Like candlesticks. And shoes..."

But he wasn't listening. He sighed and sat down at the table, cradling the bowl in his hands. "Portal creation is a long and time-honored tradition in my culture. You see our lions. You see the Empress comb. In China, we honor the knowledge of our ancestors and teach it to our young."

"Okay, fine. So you guys have turned portal creation into a science instead of an innate talent. What does that have to do with the bowl?"

"Oh, you must have talent. But if you have talent, you start off by making this. Your father never have you make a bowl, Maggie?"

"No, Xiaoming. He took me out to stake a vampire like any good father does."

Xiaoming shook his head. "You know nothing. Someday I teach you. This is a very nice bowl. It is made by a child. A child can make it. Can you make it?"

He looked at me, making sure the insult landed.

"Xiaoming, I came here for information, not your attitude."

He shook his head. "You are very angry, Maggie. You don't understand what is right and wrong about your way of thinking."

"THE BOWL, XIAOMING!"

He sighed, looking at me like I was the biggest waste of oxygen. "If you were a true student of the art of walking the worlds, you would first learn to create small cracks in the dimensions. Not big wrecking ball like you. All smashing and noise. And then you would learn to heal the portal, because world walker is no good if world walker cannot stop others from walking through worlds." He gave me another glance up and down, letting me know how I was stacking up in his mind.

"Did you read that inside a fortune cookie?" I asked.

He glared at me and lit another cigarette from the tip of the one he was smoking before snubbing out the first. "Fortune cookies made by capitalist devils like you." He pointed it at me. "I am having a moment of gratitude for the knowledge of those who came before me. Why you hate the ancestors?"

I was about to get stabby. All I wanted was to know how big our problem was. I gritted my teeth and forced myself to be pleasant. "I don't hate the ancestors, Xiaoming. In fact, I love them. I love them so much, I want to know how many bowls there are and if I need to be worried that any of them might be floating around where vampires might get them."

He shrugged. "There is no way to know."

"Listen, a shadow from the Dark Dimension tried to steal this bowl from me. And if there are things like this floating around," I picked up the bowl and waved it at him, "that leads me to believe that maybe things from that dimension are trying to get a hold of things in this dimension to create portals to bad dimensions for reasons which aren't exactly nice."

"Shadow from the Dark Dimension?" he said. "This is very bad."

"I KNOW!" I said. "That's what I've been trying to tell you."

Xiaoming sat back in his chair thoughtfully, inhaling deeply from his cigarette. Finally, he stubbed it out and said, "Okay. I will help."

"Thank you!" I said. "FINALLY."

"Finally? Why you complaining? I am helping. I could be watching my soap opera." He waved to a twelve-inch TV with tin foil attached to the antenna. An image of a woman walking sadly through a garden flickered on the screen. "But I am not. I am helping."

Heaven forbid the man should be kept from his stories because I was trying to save the world from collapse. "Thank you," I said through a forced smile.

Xiaoming grunted, pleased I had come around to seeing what a favor he was doing for me. He looked thoughtfully at the bowl. "This not able to do much. It could never open portal to Dark Dimension. That shadow who tried to steal the bowl is stupid. But if a master created something more... A master is able to open portal by ringing bowl instead of waving their hands like you."

"I don't wave my hands."

"Whatever you do."

I sighed. Gods, sometimes I hated this guy. "So, how do I destroy such a thing?"

He smiled, holding out both his hands like he had the answer to the easiest question in the world. "You break it." He then sat forward to make sure I caught the rest of his instruction. "But you must break without ringing it. If you ring it, you create permanent portal. Crack in the dimension. You mar sound without a sound, and you have a noodle bowl."

"Want to show me how?"

He grunted and shuffled into his kitchen. He filled the sink up with water and submerged the bowl. He reached under the counter and withdrew a hammer, put it under the water, and started smashing.

He then pulled up the bowl with its nice new dents and handed it over.

"May you never have a matched set, Maggie MacKay."

Chapter 11

I walked up the pathway to Mindy's house, a charming Victorian place tucked into one of the old neighborhoods in Pasadena. Her great big Irish setter was barking at me from the moment I got out of my car. It was early evening and all seemed quiet on the vampire front, which was a huge relief.

The door opened before I even knocked and I had to look down to see who was letting me in.

"Pipistrelle!" I exclaimed. "How you doing, little guy?"

Pipistrelle was the brownie who worked for my sister. My sister was thrilled to kiss housework goodbye forever. He was thrilled to have so much crown molding to dust. He gave me a bow and squeaked, "Tracker Maggie! So pleased to see you! Come in! Come in! Are you here to fight the vampires that threaten your sister's life due to your thoughtless actions?"

He obviously had been talking to my mom.

"Only if I'm lucky," I replied.

He ushered me in and shut the door.

"Hello? Anybody home?" I called.

"In here, Maggie-girl!" Dad was hanging out in the living room, looking about as comfortable lounging in Mindy's froofy parlor as he did in Mom's tea shop. Mindy's house was done in shabby-chic splendor. A place for every doily and every doily in its place.

"I'm here to relieve you of duty," I informed Dad, taking off my coat. The brownie tugged it out of my hand and it fell over his head. I went to get it off him so he could see. "Pipistrelle, give it back. You can't even reach the hangers."

Evidentially, this was not a problem. He scampered away before I could get it and shimmied up the doorjamb like a pole dancer on a Saturday night. Holding my jacket in his teeth, he made a leap for an empty hanger in a move that would have gotten him a starring role with Cirque. He straddled it and draped my coat where it was supposed to go. Then he made a leap, somersaulting in the air, and stuck the landing.

I gave him an impressed slow clap. "Perfect 10, Pipistrelle. If I had a gold medal to hand out, you would have won it."

He beamed like I actual had given him a prize and went scurrying off into the kitchen to finish up dinner. The smell of garlic and olive oil wafted through the air.

"Pipistrelle is going to make sure we are all safe from vampires tonight," I remarked as I walked into the living room.

"He does what he can," replied Dad. "See anything on the way in?"

I shook my head and flung myself into one of the chairs, dropping my overnight duffel on the floor. "Of course not. I told you, those vampires on the phone were idiots. They couldn't find their way through the boundary if there was a trail of bleeding corpses showing the way. Plus, the sun is still up."

He looked out the window. "How is that even possible? I feel like we've been sitting around here for twelve years."

"That much fun, huh?"

He gave me a knowing nod. He then looked around for mom and sat forward in his seat. The sparkle came back into his eyes. "So, did you bring the bowl?" he asked.

I reached over and pulled it out of my bag. He was rubbing his fingertips like he couldn't wait to get it back in his hands. I gave it a ting. And nothing happened.

"What happened?" he asked, looking like some sad kid watching a magician mess up.

"I made sure it got broken," I informed him.

"You did what?" he said. "We didn't even figure out what it..."

I shook my head. "Dad, first off, there is no 'we'. You're retired. Second off, this bowl is the kind of thing that will get me entirely too busy at work, especially since you're retired."

"Come on, Maggie. I might be retired but I'm not THAT retired."

"I went to Xiaoming, and evidently if you break it while it is ringing, you create a permanent portal."

Dad sat back. "Well, that is easier than the way we go around creating portals next to nuclear facilities, especially since they're closing down San Onofre."

"Yep. It sure is... I mean...was."

He gave me a disbelieving look. "You broke it before you could form us another MacKay Only portal? What kind of daughter did I raise?"

"Jeez, Dad! It is like you WANT me to go around breaking the law."

He waved it off. "Bah. We're not breaking the law! We're helping the law. In the spirit of the law. We, you and I, are making sure we have the resources we need to do our job well."

"I'M doing fine at MY job."

"Listen," he said. "I was in the tracking business for a long time and if there is one thing I've learned, you shouldn't be throwing away objects that might make your work easier. We could have made a direct portal to the Krispie Kreme in Burbank."

"You're telling me you wanted me to preserve a potentially dangerous object because you want a direct line to donuts, Dad?"

"They make a good donut."

I shook my head, calling his bluff. "No."

He sighed, tracing the embroidery on one of Mindy's pillows. "It was worth trying."

"You want to start doing 'tea' runs again, don't you?" I even gave him little air quotes around the word 'tea'. "You miss smuggling. Admit it."

After I rescued Dad, we had skirted the issue of his "delivery" days. He knew that I knew he used to smuggle vampire relicts for a fat elf who worked downtown. There was no way for me to have figured out the deal with the lion statues without putting those pieces together.

"Nah, I don't miss it," he said. "Just thinking when your mom needs you to go do errands, it doesn't make much sense for me not to do them."

I waved the bowl slowly at him. "You're as bad as an ex-smoker who asks folks to blow in his face."

"Okay. FINE." Dad flopped back in defeat. "Maybe I miss it a bit."

I picked myself up and sat down next to him, patting him on the knee. "Admitting there is a problem is the first step to recovery."

He hit me with that pillow he had been so interested in just a minute ago. "I'll give you something to recover from."

"Come on! Not the face!" I shouted, protecting myself with my hands.

Pipistrelle came running in, dragging a huge, white first aid kit behind him. "Are you in need of medical attention, Tracker Maggie?"

I gave Dad a look. "It's only fun until you freak out the brownie."

"Maggie is fine, Pipistrelle," Dad sighed, reassuring him.

Pipistrelle pushed the first aid kit against the wall. "I shall leave it here in case you need it in the immediate future." He then went skipping off.

"Wouldn't want for him to have brought it all this way for no reason, Maggie," Dad said.

I gave him a warning point to stay on his side. I picked up the bowl and handed it to him.

He turned it over sadly. "This was a pretty cool thing you ruined, Maggie."

"Xiaoming says that their world walkers have to make bowls like this when they first begin training so they can learn how to open and close portals."

"What? Shows you how talented those walkers are. You figured out portal making all on your own. You didn't need anyone to teach you pottery to push through the boundary."

I rolled my eyes, thinking back to that day in middle school I was aiming for some guy's face and ended up punching an inter-dimensional hole through two worlds instead. "Listen, since you love it so much, why don't you see if you can figure out how it worked?" I suggested. "Xiaoming said that this one was made by a kid."

"A kid?"

"A kid."

"Are you trying to give me a hobby, Maggie?" asked my dad suspiciously.

I shrugged, knowing that if I didn't get him working on something, he'd start a second career building portals to funnel cake stands. "Some people build ships in bottles, maybe you create worlds in bowls."

Chapter 12

Dad and Mom trucked off to bed around the 10 o'clock hour. Mindy and Austin followed shortly, leaving Pipistrelle to man the coffee machine for me. I probably should have called Killian to keep an eye on the back of the house for me, but the lucky bastard was off at another Solstice party. And besides, tonight's all-night gig was gratis and I didn't need to owe that elf any favors.

I heard tiny feet padding towards me and turned from my seat at the window to see what was creeping up from the kitchen. Pipistrelle's hands were full with a cappuccino mug bigger than his head.

I got up off my duff and walked over to relieve him of his burden. "Hey, little dude. I am totally set. You can go to bed now."

"I am so happy to be of service, Tracker Maggie. My gratitude for a position of such importance in the MacKay family is boundless! Just tell me what more I can do!" he said, his eyes full of hope.

"You can go to bed," I told him.

He shook his fat, round head. "Only after you give me your shoes!"

I sighed. "You can have some of your cinnamon rolls ready for me in the morning, how about that? That's a good job, right?"

"Give me your shoes!" he insisted, his face like a puppy begging for a treat.

"FINE!" I sighed as I yanked my Doc Martens off my feet.

That's the thing about brownies. One of their first recorded appearances was working with cobblers. Old habits die hard. Some people fall asleep to the sound of their television, brownies can't rest until they've nailed your soles down and spit-shined your clogs.

Pipistrelle grinned from ear-to-ear as I handed them over and hugged them tight to his chest like a favorite teddy bear. He gave me a smart salute before skipping off to his cabinet. Originally, Pipistrelle had been eyeing up the ashes in Mindy's fireplace as the perfect home away from home, but that was where she had drawn the line. Instead, she built him a little two-story apartment in one of the kitchen cupboards and furnished with her old doll furniture. Barbie never had it so good. I heard the door swing open, then shut, and then the gentle *swish swish swish* of his polish rag.

I wiggled my toes in my striped socks. As sweet as a free shoe shine was, I hoped I wouldn't have to go kicking down any doors tonight. I looked out the window at the yard. I told myself everything should be fine. Mindy's house was defended to the teeth with wards and such. I was only sitting sentry to help Mom sleep. It was just a few nights and not having to deal with her sleep deprived crankiness was more than enough to keep me on the couch scanning the skies.

Turns out Mom was right. As always. Some damn fool vampires actually did decide it was a good idea to drop by the house of the family responsible for 52% of vampire-stabbings in America. And they showed up at midnight, which makes them not just fools but fucking clichés. They landed on the sidewalk, but couldn't cross into the yard. Some people grow tulips. My sister grows garlic and wolfsbane.

I groaned and got up off the couch, giving the locks on my neck guard a pat. They weren't going to come anywhere near me, but the Boy Scouts had it right with their "always be pre-pared" motto. I picked up the meditation bowl and my stake, and walked outside.

Two young and pretty vampires were pacing the limits of Mindy's yard like tigers in a cage, except instead of testing the bars for a way out, they were looking for a way to get in. A vampire's beauty is inversely proportional to its brains and these were fucking supermodels. I reminded myself to use small words.

"Hey boys! Looking for this?" I asked, holding up the bowl.

The vampires stopped and stared at me, probably the same way we would stare at a cow if it started to talk.

"She has the bowl!" the one hissed to the other. "I told you the shadow did not succeed."

"Yeah, I nailed his ass to the wall, just like I'm getting ready to do to you." I said politely as I palmed my stake. "Any last re-quests?"

"Give us the bowl!" the second vampire hissed.

Who was I to deny a last request? "Sure!" I said and flung it at him.

He caught it and laughed with delight. "You stupid human! You have given us the power to open the hellhole!"

I leaned against Mindy's white picket fence. "Opening a hellhole, huh? No chance you're talking about a bad motel franchise opportunity?"

"We shall control the portal to the Dark Dimension! We shall rule the Earth!"

"All because of that bowl?"

"It is ours! You handed it over!"

I gave them a slow smile. "Before you celebrate too hard, give it a ding."

The vampire looked at the other and then, with his long fingernail, struck it. It rang out a pleasant little tone, but nothing happened.

"Why does it not break the boundary? Why does it merely ring?" Tweedledumber asked the other. They sat there pinging it and pinging it, as if somehow the pinging was going to connect with the dimensional wall.

"The bowl doesn't work, fellas. It's just a bowl," I called. I figured that they didn't need to know that it originally worked just fine.

"No! That is not fair! This is not the way that it was supposed to go!" the one vampire howled, throwing the bowl into the rose bushes in an epic tantrum of two-year-old-in-a-toy-store proportions.

"Yeah, life isn't fair," I replied.

The other vampire leapt forward menacingly. "We shall kill you, Maggie MacKay."

"Listen to you... whispering sweet nothings to me..." I said as I held my stake like a blushing bride with a bouquet. "We shouldn't ruin a night like this with words."

The vampire cringed back. "We were only speaking in jest! We would not kill the mighty and powerful Maggie MacKay!"

I tipped my stake at him. "Now you're speaking my language. There is nothing here of any use to you guys. This place is protected. Begone! Vamoose! Get thee to a vampirey!"

They took off down the street in a shambling run. I gave them a little finger-wave with the hand holding my stake. I walked over to the rose bushes and looked down at the bowl. "So, you were going to open up a hellhole to the Dark Dimension? And Dad was going to use you for free donuts. I'm not sure which plan was more evil."

I picked it up and walked up the stairs to the house, thanking Xiaoming in my brain that everyone could sleep soundly tonight.

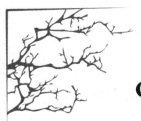

Chapter 13

When I woke in the morning, Pipistrelle had worked his magic. My shoes were inside my bedroom door looking as pretty as the day I had bought them, and the whole house smelled of cinnamon rolls and coffee. I stretched and climbed out of bed, following my nose to the kitchen.

My twin, Mindy, and her hubby, Austin, were sitting at the kitchen table reading the newspaper, all dressed up fancy for work. Her baby bump was just starting to show the hints of the MacKay-to-Come, but she was still squeezing into her old suits.

"Glad you were on duty, sis," Mindy said, not looking at me as she sipped her decaf and kept reading. "Sleep well?"

"The vampires and I came to an understanding," I replied, reaching into the cupboard for a mug. "We're cool."

"So they showed up last night?" asked Austin, flipping the page of the newspaper.

"Yep. They wanted a bowl."

"Did they get it?" asked Mindy.

"Yeah, and then they decided that didn't want it anymore."

"Mighty Maggie has vanquished the vampires and kept our home safe once more!" shouted Pipistrelle as he came into the room, balancing a basket of laundry on his head. "Hip hip hooray!"

"Do I need to hose vampire guts off the driveway?" Mindy asked, taking a bite of her cinnamon roll.

"I would be honored to clean vampire entrails for the Mighty Maggie!" volunteered Pipistrelle.

I slowed him down. "It's okay, Pipistrelle. We just talked. I showed them that the bowl doesn't do anything and they went away."

"Really? You let them go?" asked Austin, pausing for the first time to look at me.

"Needed them to let the rest of their hive know that there was nothing here for them."

Austin nodded and then went back to the paper. "Do you have the crossword, Mindy?"

"Mmm-hmmm," she replied. "Almost done with it. What's a six-letter word for 'dumbass'? It starts with a 'M.'"

"Ha ha," I replied. "Violence isn't the answer to everything."

Mindy put down her paper and gave me a look. "Austin? The vampires got my sister. I don't know this woman."

"Who don't you know?" asked Dad as he shuffled into the kitchen, yawning and ruffling his grey-blonde bed head. He took my coffee out of my hands and drank it.

"My twin," replied Mindy. "Vampires showed up last night and she let them walk away."

Dad did a spit-take. "She did WHAT?!?"

I went over to the cupboard and poured myself another cup. "It is NOTHING. Really."

"I don't think vampires are nothing, Maggie," pointed out Dad.

"As I was telling Mindy, they wanted the bowl to create a hellhole to the Dark Dimension. I needed to show them that we didn't have the bowl they were looking for and then have them spread the word among their friends."

"Oh." Dad sat back, mopping the coffee off his front. "Great coffee, Pipistrelle!"

Pipistrelle gave him a little thumbs-up and then went off to the laundry room.

"DAD," Mindy whined, "Maggie put my life in danger again."

"Maggie, stop putting your sister's life in danger," Dad said as he reached for a cinnamon roll. "Now, what was that about a hellhole?"

"Dunno the details. It's on my to-do list today."

"Well, let me know if there is anything I can do to help."

"Actually," I said, "Any chance you could bump up your new bowl-hobby to a full-on obsession? I'm thinking it might be smart to figure out how that thing worked."

"You told me last night I'm retired."

"DAAAAAD," I pleaded.

"Fine. I'll make you a portal to the Dark Dimension using tableware. Will that make you happy?"

I gave him a kiss on the cheek and stole his cinnamon roll. "Divinely."

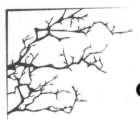

Chapter 14

"Killian!" I said, shaking his boot. "We got a job!"

"No more gargoyles!" he muttered, half awake, half asleep at his desk. Evidently, the build up to Solstice was still going strong.

I smiled and patted his shoulder. "No more gargoyles."

Killian rose from his seat and stretched. "What?"

"No more gargoyles!" I repeated. "We got a new job!"

He grinned. "You are not jesting? We have a job? A real job?"

"Real...ish."

He looked at me suspiciously. "What does that mean, Maggie?"

"Why are you looking at this gift horse in the teeth?" I asked. "Here we have a job that involves zero chisels and zero church climbing..."

Killian shook his head. "Why do I think you are not telling me everything?"

"Because you are a grumpy old man who has been working too hard for too long. What do you say we start taking down some bad guys?" I suggested, motioning towards the door.

He wandered over to the kitchenette to pour himself a cup of joe. "Any particular reason why we should start now?"

"Hey, today is as good as any!"

"You are so very cheerful about this new opportunity, Maggie," Killian said with a wry laugh. He pointed his mug at my empty hands. "If we have a job, why do you not have a folder from Frank?"

He was entirely too observant for someone with an ambrosia hangover.

"I left it in the car," I lied.

Killian came over, stepping uncomfortably close into my personal space. We were now in a game of chicken to see who blinked first. He brushed back a strand of my black hair and stared at me deep into my eyes. "You are terrible at untruths."

"No, I'm not."

"Do you find me attractive?"

"No."

He waved his finger in my face. "A terrible liar." He sat down on the edge of his desk and put his mug down beside him. "Go on, Maggie. Tell me what depth of hell you expect me to descend to, all in the name of the greater good."

"Funny you should mention hell..."

"What about hell, Maggie?"

"Vampires..." I stalled.

"Vampires, what?" he asked, cupping his ear. "I did not quite catch the rest of that?"

"Vampires want to open a hellhole to the Dark Dimension."

"You are mumbling, Maggie. It sounds as if you said that vampires wanted to open a hellhole to the Dark Dimension."

I stared at the ceiling. "I did."

"And I suppose you want us, with our struggling new business and valuable, billable hours, to turn away from new clients to stop the vampires? For fun?"

"Yes."

He got up and got his coat and headed towards the door. He looked back at me. "Well? Come along then. Let us go save the world." He booped me on the nose and gave me a smile. "Again."

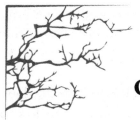

Chapter 15

Killian and I bounced from the Other Side to downtown Hollywood by late-afternoon. June gloom was hanging over the city. Or maybe just smog. But the streets were filled with summer tourists. As we sat waiting for the crosswalk on Hollywood and Highland to clear, I was doing the math on how many years I'd get in the clink if I rid the world of some of its pedestrians. True, no one walks in LA, but these folks shouldn't even be *allowed* to walk in LA. I laid on my horn. "Quit snapping pictures of the Hollywood sign and move your dumb ass!"

"Where are we going, Maggie?"

"To church."

I flipped off a family wearing color-coordinated t-shirts who couldn't coordinate their feet to get out of my way.

"You are a beacon of spirituality," Killian replied.

"We're not going for me," I said.

"Perhaps we should."

"We're going to visit Father Killarney."

Killian looked at me with a cold stare. "You swore that this personal project involved no chisels or climbing."

"It doesn't! I double swear. We're not picking up his gargoyles. It's just that if anyone knows about gates to the Dark Dimension, it's probably Father Killarney."

"More than your father?"

"Dad never messed with that side of the boundary," I informed him prudishly. "We were strict Earth-to-Other-Siders. Also, Dad is already busy building us a portal there."

"He is?" said Killian. "This cannot end well."

"Don't get your tights in a wad. He's just trying to figure out how it is done. Xiaoming looked at the bowl and then I broke it so the vampires wouldn't eat my family and now I need my dad to figure out how to put it back together again."

"Why do you not just return to Xiaoming for this information?"

I laughed. "Guess who has two thumbs, is concealing two guns, and just learned how to delegate?" I pointed at me. "It's all on Dad now."

He shook his head. "Why not simply kill the vampires, Maggie?"

"Believe it or not, I think this is the easier way."

He placed a hand upon my forehead. "Are you ill?"

"What is it with you people?! It's like a girl can't go around deciding that she doesn't want to stake someone without you acting like she's gone insane."

"Have you gone insane?"

"No," I snapped. "Jesus..."

"Speaking of..." interrupted Killian, "turn left for the church..."

"I know where I'm going, elf." Elves usually don't ride in cars and I was starting to think maybe it was less personal preference and more a moratorium based upon their backseat driving.

But I turned left.

The sidewalk was packed. There were people everywhere. I wondered what was going on.

"Why would a religious leader like Father Killarney have knowledge of the Dark Dimension?" Killian asked.

I started looking around for parking and spotted a lot up ahead. "Some of these spiritual do-gooders and religious types get into the business because they can sense evil and need to know how to stop it," I replied, creeping the car forward. "When it comes to humans having any protections at all, all of this fibberty-flabberty comes down to some of humanity's first wards. Holy water, rituals, exorcisms… they were the ones who figured out how to close up the hellholes in the first place."

"Really?"

"Really. They are ever-vigilant, seeking out evil and tearing it out by the roots."

"How is it that you sense evil so acutely, Maggie, living your life as you do without any trace of religion, spirituality, or the urge to do good?"

"I am truly blessed."

We pulled past Father Killarney's church. There were booths and food trucks, a bouncy house and those blow-up sumo suits, a Ferris wheel and every manner of barf-mobile ride in the lot.

My heart clenched in dread. "Oh god."

Killian looked back at the odd blend of garish colors against the church's stucco walls. "What? Is something wrong? Are you sensing some form of evil?"

"This is worse than evil, Killian. It is the church carnival."

Chapter 16

A dad waved us into the lot using his kid's toy light-up sword. Come to think of it, this being Hollywood, the sword might have been his. The lot was full of moms in their frilly flowered dresses, dads in their khakis and polos... and us. Me in my black leathers and Killian in casual elfin wear.

"We gotta buy you a pair of pants," I said as I shut off the car.

"Perhaps today was not the best day to visit Father Killarney," Killian observed as a fellow in pink shirt-sleeves and a comb-over passed by.

"You think? Jesus. What day is today?" I asked, trying to figure out if I could get my parking money back if we left now.

"Sunday," said Killian, getting out of the car.

"Oh, man..." I replied, sinking my forehead against the steering wheel.

"What is it?" he asked.

"It's the human day of deity worship," I reminded him. I got out of the car and slammed the door. "Everything should have been done hours ago, but we've hit it on the parish carnival weekend." The sound of laughing children tinkled across the paved asphalt. "I'm about as comfortable at these things as a cat in a baptismal fount."

"Oh look!" Killian exclaimed with delight, pointing at one of the signs. "A pancake breakfast! And darts!"

"You're as bad as Pipistrelle, Killian. This is not fun," I glowered.

Killian slung his arm over my shoulders. "This is great amounts of fun. I have to say, Maggie, I was unsure about your suggested plan of attack, but I am finding myself more and more agreeable. Do you think that evil is behind those cans of milk bottles people are trying to knock over?"

"No! I don't——" but the elf was already laying his, a.k.a. my, money down. He fired off his shots and knocked down those milk bottles so fast that the carnie never knew what hit him.

"Not bad, elf," I said, slightly impressed.

"Which prize do you think is the most fearsome?" he asked. "The orange elephant or the pink tiger?"

"You're not carrying around a pink tiger," I informed him.

"Orange elephant it is!" he said, reaching out his hands like a toddler who just learned 'gimme'.

"Are you selectively dense?" I asked him.

"Ooo! Kids! Look! They're from *The Hobbit*!" someone shouted.

"God, I hate costumed characters," I muttered before realizing that they were coming straight for us. "We need to go. Now!" I said as I tried to drag Killian away.

But he was already wrapping his arms around the kiddos and smiling his face off. There were so many camera-phones flashing, you'd think Beyoncé had come to town. I could hardly wait to see how many family Christmas cards Killian would be gracing this year.

"This is a wonderful celebration, Maggie!" he said after he had finished with his paparazzi. "I did not know that the Catholics celebrate Solstice."

"They don't."

He looked around in wonder. "You mean this is a part of their ordinary religious celebrations? I shall have to send an update to my Earth's Religions professor and have the textbook updated."

"Church festivals aren't—" I knew it was no use. Killian was as high on life as a kid on cotton candy. I'd dash his dreams later. "Can we find Father Killarney?"

"Do you believe Father Killarney might be next to that cupcake truck?" he asked before loping off.

"Killian..." I shouted after him.

He turned back, mystified. "Where is your sense of fun, Maggie?"

"I stabbed it. I stabbed my fun the first time I staked a vampire. Speaking of which," I grabbed his arm and directed him away from the cupcakes and more towards the rectory, "we need to find Father Killarney so we can find out what other things I can look forward to stabbing."

Killian stopped. "You want my orange elephant, don't you?"

"I DON'T WANT YOUR ELEPHANT!"

"It is okay." He put it in my arms. "Take this one. I shall win myself another."

"Oh, feckin' toads on a pogo stick," came a familiar Irish brogue. I turned around and there was Father Killarney. Guess he got the memo that this wasn't a social call. "So the vampires are off to ruin my life again, is it? Haven't they had enough?"

"Evidently, not," I replied, giving him a hug. "How did you know?"

"That father of yours gave me a ring, asking me about creating portals to Dark Dimensions and vampires visiting you again at night. And then I come out here and see you're ruining our parish festival."

"That's about the speed of things."

"Why don't you come inside where we can talk without scaring away my flock?" Father Killarney looked down at the bundle of polyester joy in my arms. "Oh, did that elf of yours win you a prize, Maggie-girl?" he asked.

"I'm just holding it for him," I muttered, glaring at Killian.

"Sure, sure... just holdin' a man's orange elephant. Quite generous of you," he said with a wink and a nudge.

I shoved the elephant into Killian's arms. "Don't make me rip you a new portal."

Killian turned to Father Killarney. "She is just embarrassed she did not win it herself."

"I didn't even try to win one!" I shouted as the boys nodded their heads in understanding. "I didn't even want one in the first place!"

Father Killarney took the elephant from Killian and handed it back to me. "Now Maggie, be polite and take the man's elephant."

I hit Killian with his own stuffed animal. "I hope you are happy."

Killian grinned as he watched me storm. "This sight is causing me exceeding amounts of joy."

We followed Father Killarney into his rectory and sat across the desk from him. "So, what is it exactly that made you drive all the way out to Hollywood on a Sunday? It is a shame it was not for my homily, because it was an excellent one, if I do say so myself."

"It's because of those vampires. I need information on opening doors to the Dark Dimension."

"What sort of world are we living in, Maggie, when a parish priest is teaching his flock how to open portals to Hell?"

"This world?"

"It is not a world I want to be a part of," said Father Killarney. "Opening up a portal to the Dark Dimension is inviting a horrifying evil. Why, the angels in heaven themselves closed that door for our own good and survival. The knowledge that there are even doors to such a terrible place should be lost to the ravages of time, much less the knowledge that someone is actually capable of opening them."

"Speaking of which, any idea how you do it?"

"No! No, I do not, Maggie! How dare you!"

I gave him a look.

"Fine. Yes. I know the stories. But don't you think you are going to be getting them out of me, Maggie MacKay."

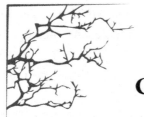

Chapter 17

"Hellholes..." Father Killarney rubbed his beard and took a big swallow off the top of his pint. "You realize what you're asking me."

We were sitting in Father Killarney's favorite pub. This guy was going to drink a hole through my pocket, but I'd learned long ago the best way to an Irish man's heart is through his liver.

"I have absolutely no clue what I'm asking you," I replied, motioning to the bartender to keep the rounds coming. "I take it that this is a bigger deal than directions to In-n-Out."

"This is not directions to a fast-food restaurant, Maggie."

"They do make a wicked burger."

"Their burgers will not destroy you."

"Says you. You should see what they've done to my pant-size." I could see he was losing patience with me. I reached out and gripped his hand. "I promise I am only asking this to ensure humanities' survival."

"If I tell you, there may not be any humans left to survive."

"I promise I won't use the information against our species."

Father Killarney sighed and drained his glass. Killian had the new pint from the bartender on the table even before Father Killarney put down the empty. We made a great team.

Father Killarney wiped his bristly lips. "All right, Maggie, it is upon your own soul. Yours and your partner's. I'll not take responsibility for it."

"I'll take my chances."

He looked at Killian. "You, too?"

Killian looked a little less convinced but sort of shrugged half-heartedly. "I am sure Maggie will repay me a favor for my soul, if necessary."

"I never agreed to that, Killian," I pointed out.

He shrugged again.

"How about I just promise to buy you fries from McDryads?"

"That would also be agreeable."

We shook on it.

I turned back to Father Killarney. "Okay, get going."

He nodded, seemingly contented with whatever deal we had worked out between the two of us. "You know all the stories about the forces of good and evil, the battles between the angels, with Lucifer being cast out of heaven?"

"The only part of Sunday school I didn't sleep through," I replied proudly.

He leaned forward. "The truth of it is more complicated. This was back in the day before even the dinosaurs roamed the Earth. This planet was nothing but a molten ball of brimstone and fire. It was a time when there was no boundary between the Earth and the Dark Dimension. They were one and the same."

"How long ago was all this?" I asked.

"Geologically? Early Precambrian."

"I don't know what that means."

"Four billion years ago," he said. "Give or take a hundred-million. The battles were terrible, every day practically a nuclear holocaust. That's when the boundary was created. Those creatures of death and fire were confined to the Dark Dimension. This planet, finally left to its own devices, had the space and time for life to take hold. Those ancient World Walkers who created the boundary placed the Other Side between Earth and the Dark Dimension as a buffer. They hoped it would be too difficult to crossover. Do you understand what I'm saying to you, Maggie-girl?"

"Not yet," I replied, chewing on an onion ring, trying my best to look thoughtful.

"When you create a portal to the Dark Dimension, you are breaking through two boundaries. You are destroying the will of those who sought to protect the world. That's not a thing to take lightly."

I shrugged. "Listen, Father, I'm not the one who wants to build the Lincoln Tunnel of Evil. And by Lincoln Tunnel of Evil, I'm not talking to New Jersey. The vampires are at the hardware store of destruction and I gotta figure out why."

"Also who, when, and where," Killian added.

"Those, too," I agreed. "'How' would also be nice."

Father Killarney downed his second pint. Good thing his church was within stumbling distance. "Vampires are creatures of the Dark Dimension, Maggie. The ones you fight? They are wayfaring wanderers that somehow managed to get through. But open up a portal to the Dark Dimension? Why, who knows how many of their brethren live in that world..."

"But why build the portal to Earth?" I asked, trying for the love of mike to figure out the vampire logic. "If they've got a hankering for some sort of cosmic family reunion, why not just open up a portal in the Other Side, pour through, and be done with it?"

He shook his head. "There are too many powers on the Other Side to contain them. Earth is practically defenseless. It is filled with humans fattened and at the ready like a ranch of turkeys before Thanksgiving. Why storm the castle when there is a veritable slaughterhouse at your fingertips?"

"Ugh. So the lazy slobs are looking for easy pickings?" I said.

"Wouldn't you if you had a whole dimension of hungry mouths to feed?" asked Father Killarney.

Killian got us both back on track. "Suppose the vampires of the Dark Dimension do manage to build this hellhole. Does the Earth have any defense against it?"

"Only thing that can stop up a hellhole is for someone like Maggie here," Father Killarney said pointing at me, "to find a way to close it."

I smiled. "Cool. So our chances are looking up, since I'm more like Maggie than anyone I know."

"Maggie," said Father Killarney seriously, "you and your father may be the most gifted World Walkers our worlds have seen in a blessed age, but the creatures of the Dark Dimension have been testing every square inch of the Boundary since the dawn of time trying to get out. If there is an open portal, I fear they will begin rushing through. It is not a case of just letting the portal close itself. You will need to weld that dimension shut."

"What? Move fast and weld shut a portal? Listen, Father, I have got it covered. You're talking to the dimensional equivalent of that chick from *Flashdance*."

"I don't think you know what you're biting off here, Maggie."

"I can handle it!" I insisted. "Sheesh. It's like you don't even know what I do every day."

"This is not like what you face every day, Maggie."

"You've gotten soft," I said dismissively as I took a sip of my pint.

Killian again stopped us both. "Father, to get back to my question, in the event that Maggie... not that I believe she is even capable of failing... but in the event the portal opens while we are engaged elsewhere..."

Killian was sweetly tap dancing his way around that minefield. I should get the elf a job at the U.N.

"...what protections are available for the people of the Earth?" he asked. "Is there some sort of object or creature or anything which might be of help?"

I added, "I can get work permits."

"Oh, I don't know," said Father Killarney, leaning back in his seat and staring at the ceiling. "These hellholes are things of legends. Back in the day, there were stories of angels with wings and halos beating back the forces of darkness. The saints and their relics. Gargoyles upon the eaves."

Father Killarney, Killian, and I looked at one another.

"You just said gargoyles."

"Shit," I said.

"Now, Maggie, maybe this is just a coincidence," he said.

"You know it is not."

"Gargoyles have always been friends to the church," he pointed out.

"Tell me another bedtime story."

"How many gargoyles have gathered around your church?" Killian asked.

"At least a hundred," said Father Killarney, who then drained his glass again.

I motioned to the bartender for a round of shots and knocked mine back the moment it hit the table. I wiped my mouth with the back of my hand. "Can I talk to your gargoyles?"

"I'll get the keys to the shed," he said, standing up. He pushed his drink my direction.

When a priest thinks you need something to steady your constitution, you know you're in for a lousy night.

I reached for it but Killian beat me to it. He picked it up and downed it.

"Hey!" I said.

He pointed his finger at me. "You said that this job would not involve gargoyles."

I pushed the last remaining shot his direction. "Go for it. I owe you."

He didn't fight me. It was going to be a really, really lousy night.

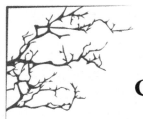

Chapter 18

By the time we stumbled back to the church, the carnival had shuttered up for the night and the place was pretty well deserted. Father Killarney gave a couple of friendly hand-shakes to some hangers on and assured them they had worked so hard all day, they should go home now, and he'd handle the rest.

I didn't know a man of God could lie so well.

"I'll be glad when we've finished the restoration work," he muttered as he moved a paint bucket off the steps and opened the door to the rectory. "You try to fix just a few cracks in the front steps and suddenly you're replacing all the wires and plumbing."

He came back with the keys to the shed. He put them in my hand and closed my fingers around them. "God be with you, Maggie. I hope that this is not what we fear it might be."

That made two of us. I looked over at Killian. Scratch that, three.

Father Killarney disappeared to shoo the last remaining people off the property and lock up the gates for the night. We certainly didn't need any tourists wandering in while we had ourselves a little sit-down with a bunch of animated stones.

The sun dipped down behind the mountains and slowly the sky went all pretty and pink, then faded to scary blue and black. Killian looked at me and I looked at him. There was no putting this off. Game on.

I walked over to the shed and unlocked the side door. As the moonlight filled the place, the gargoyles slowly starting coming to, crumbling out of their stony exterior and shaking off the dust.

"Oh, so it's the tracker," said one as he elbowed his friend.

I tried not to scream. Jesus, they are fucking terrifying.

Their teeth were the size of Ginsu knives, their talons looked like meat cleavers. Their voices rattled at that perfect pitch between nails on a chalkboard and a train barreling down the track as your car is stalled on the crossing. They moved like a pride of lions in the grass. I was reminded that I was just a big pile of meat walking around on two legs and someone was hungry.

"Hey guys!" My hand shook as I waved.

"What can we do for you? Or should we start running now?" asked a fat one with buggy eyes, elbowing his buddy.

I swallowed and tried to play it cool, pretending like my stomach wasn't about to empty its contents all over Killian's shoes. "Listen, we were wondering if we could help you...?"

All those gargoyles looked at me and, in unison, cocked their heads like dogs trying to figure out the ball-and-fetch idea.

At that moment, the door slammed shut behind us and a bone-chilling laugh crackled through the room.

The spell was broken. The buggy one gave a shrug. "Looks like we're on duty, Jeff."

"Looks like."

There was barely time to think. Killian and I instinctively ducked as, in a rustle of bat-like wings, they flung open the door to the shed and poured out like a raging river. Killian and I stood and strode out behind them.

It was another shadow, only this one was big. It was huge. It was like a black building with claws flickering in and out of the uneven yellow of the street lights.

"Shadows are slipping through," I muttered under my breath to Killian. "They must be little cracks between the boundaries that flat critters like them can squeeze through."

We stood there watching from the doorway as the gargoyles took down the bad spirit like pit bulls on a bear. I unholstered my silver-packed gun and took aim.

"Back off, tracker! This one is ours!" Jeff shouted at me from the sky.

"You sure?" I yelled back. "I'm happy to help!"

"Stay out of our way!" he replied. "We have ourselves what we call a blue-plate special! We got this covered!"

Actually, I was thrilled to pieces they had this covered. That dark spirit was a fucking nightmare. As in, I really think he might be a nightmare. The creatures from the Dark universe feed off of lots of different things. I mean, most of them feed off of fear, but some liked the fear of scaring a person when awake, some preferred it when they were asleep. Sleep made for easy pickin's. I'm pretty sure I recognized this guy as a nightmare. It was hard to tell, though, because the gargoyles had already eaten his face.

Boy, I was really glad they were on my side.

Moments later it was all over. The evil spirit was gone and the gargoyles were sitting on the basketball backboard and anywhere else they could roost, flossing their teeth with their talons, and cleaning themselves like cats, legs up and all. One of them gave a loud burp and patted his fat tummy.

"So, what was that about helping us?" asked the buggy one.

"Sorry, I didn't catch your name," I said as I re-holstered my gun. I started to stick out my hand to shake and then thought better of it. "I'm Maggie. This is Killian." Killian gave a half-hearted wave. "We're friends of Father Killarney."

"I'm Arturo. You met Jeff." The other guy waved back. "Over there is Bernard, Spike, Maude, Peaseblossom..." He kept going on. Around name twenty I was completely zoned out. Their voices made me want to crawl out of my skin. I tried to remind myself that they were the good guys. When he finally finished the introductions, they were all pretty much finished recovering from their monster snack. Jeff wiped his mouth and grinned.

"Pleasure to meet you... all of you..." I said. Killian was pale and shaky beside me, but nodded politely.

"Pleasure? We must be losing our touch, Arturo!" joked one of the gargoyles.

Fantastic. I had comedians.

"Listen," I said. "I noticed that there are a bunch of you guys here... I mean that in a gender neutral way, no offense Maude..."

She gave me a 'whatsup' nod with her chin.

"Didn't know if there was a reason you were hanging around or if the rent was just low...?

"We're here to protect that priest of yours," said Arturo. "Good man. Lots of soul."

"He'll be thrilled to hear he and his flock keeps you comfortable," I replied.

"Bad stuff is going down here soon, Maggie," Maude continued.

"Any idea what? Specifically?"

"Vampires."

When was the answer not vampires? Never. The answer is never not vampires.

"Except," said Killian, raising his finger to make a point, "that attack you just defended the church from was not a vampire. It was a shadow."

I turned back to the gargoyles. "Any ideas why that nightmare decided to pounce upon this church?"

"You don't know?" asked Jeff incredulously.

I looked over at the gargoyle sharply. "Know what?"

He looked at his buddy and elbowed him in the ribs. "She doesn't know. World Walker Tracker Maggie is off hunting the bad guys to the end of the earth and she doesn't know about this place."

"WHAT about this place?" I asked.

"Feel it!" said Arturo, spreading his arms out wide. "We're standing on one of the biggest vortexes in the world."

I never thought to 'feel it' before. It wasn't particularly a muscle I liked stretching to see how many horrible ways it could flex unless I knew absolutely what was waiting across the boundary for us. The one time I had ripped a hole in the dimensions around here, we had ended up in the elfin forest. That was all the info I needed. But, I gently nudged around a bit to see what else was there. "Shit."

So, okay: I operate on Earth and The Other Side, there's the Dark Dimension, but there are other dimensions, too. Dimensions that are seriously not as scenic as what I take for

granted, places you do not want to be late at night if you're not
seriously armed. Vortexes are all over Earth and some of them
line up to the Other Side, like the lovely little ones I like to pop
in and out of. And then some of them are crossroads to a bunch
of spots. Like the one that was evidently all around us.

"Where does it go?"

"To Hell."

"No, seriously," I said. "You're telling me that the hellhole
that the vampires want to rip open is right here?"

Jeff laughed, and it was awful. "Why else do you think the
church was built here?"

Arturo continued the thought. "It was meant to plug up
the hole. But now, the vampires are coming over to unclog the
drain."

"You're saying that these vampires are the multiverse's
great, big, undead toilet plunger?"

"Just a little push, a little pull, and they're through."

"Fuck," I said, the pieces all starting to fit together. "Listen,
you help me out with this and consider yourselves permanent
guests of the United States of America whenever retrieval paperwork comes across my desk."

The gargoyles looked at one another, like they were talking,
but I couldn't hear them. Finally, Arturo replied. "That sounds
like quite a deal."

Just then, the sky darkened as the moon was blotted out. It
looked like a swarm of demons. At least I think they looked like
a swarm of demons. Killian had his collapsible staff out before I
could even blink. Someday I was going to get him to teach me
that trick.

The gargoyles, meanwhile, looked at the demons as happy as Killian had at the prospect of the carnival's cupcakes. The gargoyles were beginning to lift off to take off after their evening prey.

"What can we do to aid you?" Killian shouted as they went.

Arturo stopped in midflight, hovering in the air. "We need reinforcements. We're rounding up all the gargoyles we can, but you keep snatching them and taking them back to the Other Side," he yelled.

"I didn't know!" I called to him lamely.

"Well, if you could go bring back some friends, that would be swell! We could use an army for this!"

Jeff came whizzing by. Killian cupped his hands to his mouth. "Are you sure that you and your army will be able to hold the border?"

The gargoyle snorted, which caused fire to shoot out of his nose. "I've been holding borders since your mom was braiding daisy chains."

"I'm several hundred years old," Killian shouted back.

"Give me a call when you hit your first epoch, elf. Otherwise, I'm underwhelmed."

And then he was gone. Killian and I just stood there for a moment in the silence, letting our neck hairs go down and the fear to fade.

Finally, I let out a big sigh of relief. "Okay, Killian," I said. "We have our marching orders."

Killian followed me. "Nice fellows," he remarked. "Not so scary when you get to know them. They remind me a lot of you."

I socked him in the arm, but my heart wasn't in it. As I watched those scary guys fly off to battle a sky full of even scarier guys, I just wanted to hug the man next to me and pretend this wasn't happening.

So I punched him instead, harder, right in the same spot.

Killian laughed and put his arm around me. "Me, too," he said, and walked us to the car.

Chapter 19

Killian and I drove up the Pacific Coast Highway. The ocean was on the left side of the road, the soft foothills of the Golden State were on the other. The smell of salty seawater mixed with sage and eucalyptus. I had an inkling where the tribe of gargoyles hung out on the Other Side. Unfortunately, no roads lead there. The gargoyles' desire to be left alone would make Greta Garbo seem like an attention whore. So, rather than spending three months hiking through inhospitable, troll-infested territory, I made the executive decision that we should drive as far as we could go on Earth, where the toughest creatures you're going to run into are some locals protecting their surf spots, and then rip an illegal portal for us through the boundary. Dad would be so proud. As he used to say, "What's the use of being a World Walker if you don't walk through some worlds?"

I pulled off the road and parked the car on the shoulder. I'm sure in other places in America, they frown on using a highway as a lot, but we were pretty well hidden among all the other dudes and dudettes taking a break from driving to see how warm the waters of the Pacific were today. The sound of the waves crashed. The sun was shining. God, I hated that this was a work trip.

I walked around to the passenger side of the car where the hill would keep us from prying eyes. Killian finished grabbing some gear from my dented trunk and gave me a nod.

I pushed my hand through the border and the landscape shimmered. Plunging my arm into the boundary looks almost like someone reaching into a lake, only instead of water, my arm had disappeared beneath the surface of the air. I felt that instant putty, that walled pressure. This was not a thin spot. The border so did not want to be opened, but I kept teasing and stretching until there was a portal big enough to climb through.

"Ready for ya, Killian," I grunted.

He picked up both our packs, since I was a little distracted at the moment, and hopped through. I followed behind him and let the portal close.

It was like we had stepped into another world. Well, because we had. Yes, there was still ocean crashing upon a rocky shore and seagulls rang out above our heads, but it was a cold beach. The entire world was colored in shades of grey. The double suns of the Other Side cast almost no light here, blocked out by the thick fog blowing in from an ocean you never wanted to go swimming in.

I leaned my hands on my thighs as I bent over, feeling winded. I felt like I had just sprinted a mile.

"Are you well, Maggie?" Killian asked with some concern, coming over to rub my back.

I nodded grimly, keeping my head down so that I didn't pass out. "Yep. Just checking my shoelaces."

Killian reached down and untied my bow. "It is a good thing you paused to check. Perhaps you should sit while you retie it."

I laughed. The elf had my number. I plopped down on the ground and breathed in deep, getting my first look around.

I could hear the mermaids singing in the distance. I double-checked Killian to make sure he wouldn't go throwing himself in to the water after some tail. Looked like the fish folk and the fairy folk don't mix, though, because he seemed more annoyed than hot and heavy.

"Have they no shame?" he muttered under his breath. "It is not even three o'clock."

"Really, Killian?" I laughed incredulously. "This coming from the man who will glamour anything with two legs no matter where the suns are in the sky?"

"Two legs," he pointed out to me, holding up his fingers to clarify. "Not 'no legs.'"

"Come on," I said, standing up and waving at him to follow me. "I'll let you get a good look at my two legs if it will put you in a better mood."

"A generous offer, Maggie," he replied.

"Well, figure you'll have nowhere else to look as we crawl up the side of this bluff."

We stood humbled beneath the sharp granite cliffs of the Other Side.

"I wish you had worn a skirt," he replied dryly.

"Just not your lucky day."

He sighed, the cliff face rising at least six stories above us before it disappeared into the clouds. "So, your intelligence and instincts led you to believe that the gargoyle tribe lives at the top of these cliffs, Maggie?" Killian asked, shading his eyes to see the top.

"Yep."

"Are you sure?" he replied.

The fog parted. I tried not to pee my pants. "Yep. I'm pretty sure that my intelligence and instincts were spot on."

There were a fucking million gargoyles on that cliff. And they were all awake. See, gargoyles are powered by the moon, and the Earth's moon has about as much voltage as an AAA battery, so they shut down when the moon goes to bed and the sun comes out to say hello. But we weren't on Earth. We were on the Other Side, and the Other Side moon is a power plant. One moon bath and you've got enough magical charge to disco all day and all night. So, here we were, about to climb up into the den, with all the beasties wide awake. They were just nested up there like sea birds, gallivanting around like a bunch of mountain goats. A shower of rocks came down on us as one of the gargoyles hit an outcropping with his wing.

"Boy, I wish they were asleep," I muttered.

"It makes me long for the days we were chiseling them off cathedral eaves," Killian replied.

"Maybe we could lure them to earth, turn them to stone, and then line them up for a nice friendly chat once the moon rises?" I suggested.

"I do not believe that luring them anywhere shall make our duties easier, Maggie," Killian replied.

"It could," I protested.

"No."

I heaved a sigh, looking up at that massive face of the bluff. "Have I mentioned how much I don't want to do this?" I asked.

"You should have mentioned it louder," replied Killian as he held up the climbing rope. "I would have listened."

I took it. "Have I mentioned that elves are so much better at climbing than humans?"

"This seems like the perfect opportunity for you to improve your skills, Maggie. I would happily hold the bottom of the ladder."

Fucking elf.

We geared up and got the pins inserted into the first spot. Slowly, we began climbing our way up. The gargoyles were staring down at us and hissing. Small bits of rock and stone bounced off my helmet.

"Come on, you bastards, I'm on your side! I just need to talk to you!" I shouted as I shielded my face with my forearm.

A gargoyle came swooping down, his leathery wings beating the air like something out of a nightmare. He got right next to my face and let out a mighty roar. It was like a dragon. Or a T. rex. I definitely had the sensation that I was about to become lunch. I desperately clawed my way through the empty closets of my mind and came up with the only prayer I could think of. "Now I lay me down to sleep..."

The gargoyle cocked his head to the side and sort of looked at me as I kept repeating it over and over again.

"You'll have to actually mean the prayer if you want me not to eat you," he growled.

"Listen, dude, I don't want you to eat me. I need your help," I said, barely opening my eyes to look at him.

"And why do you desecrate our most sacred home?"

"I promise it is really, really important," I said cringing. "I just really need to talk to your leader. Really."

The gargoyle laughed. Oh, that laugh. It was like nails on a chalkboard, if the chalkboard is your face and the nails are hot acid. He pointed a fat claw to the top of the cliffs. "If you can climb to the top, we might see about allowing you to talk to 'our leader.'"

"Are you kidding me?" I muttered, looking up in fear.

"We do not jest."

And with that, the gargoyle flew off. The rain of stones continued. My hands were bloodied from where a particularly sharp rock hit them. But I could tell that the gargoyles weren't out to destroy us quite yet. I mean, they probably would get around to it here shortly, but for the moment, I think their curiosity was getting the better of them and they figured they'd let us live long enough to get the details. And then probably fling us over the edge so we'd be good and scared when they chewed on us in midair.

But we made it. FINALLY. We didn't die, and that was feeling like a pretty massive victory in my book. Killian and I climbed over the top of the cliff and stood panting, taking in our surroundings. The expanse before us was broad and dead. The gargoyles jumped from boulder to boulder, chomping on stones and playing with each other, which sounded like a bunch of rocks wresting because that's what was actually going on. Gargoyles are nothing but animated rocks. With rock-teeth. I was so screwed if this didn't work.

"Um... I'm here to talk to your leader," I announced, stepping forward with far more bravery than I was feeling at the moment.

All of the gargoyles stopped and stared and then began to laugh.

"We are all the leader," said the gargoyles in one voice. And then they all began to advance upon Killian and me.

Fuck.

"Well, listen, before you smoosh us, can we just sit down and have a conversation?" I offered.

They did not sit down.

"Anything, Killian?" I muttered out of the corner of my mouth.

He pulled out his staff, his eyes wide. "My people are one with the living nature. We do not deal with those of the ungrowing earth and stone."

"I should have gotten myself a dwarf."

"I wish you had gotten a dwarf."

The gargoyles were herding us back to the lip of the cliff. My guess about being tossed to our death was probably not very far off.

"Father Killarney sent me!" I shouted.

That stopped them.

"Father Killarney!" I shouted again. "Nice priest! You know him, right? Father Killarney? He sent me!"

"You know Father Killarney?" one of the guys in the front said.

Killian nodded his head furiously as I reassured them. "Yes, we work together all the time. ALL THE TIME."

"We are engaged by him for this most sacred quest!" Killian added. "A holy duty which has brought us! We trespass in your home because the situation is most dire!"

It seemed like they were starting to soften towards Killian, but the jury still seemed to be out on me. "And what is your name, human?"

"Maggie. Maggie MacKay," I stammered.

They growled as one. "You forcibly removed our people from their posts."

I guess this is what they mean by don't burn any bridges you might need to cross later. I tried to explain. "I didn't know you guys were trying to keep the world from imploding, okay? I thought you were breaking Other Side law and were trying to rain chaos down upon the Earth. You don't like chaos, right?" Their hive minds seemed to chew on that a bit. "Listen, I promise to lose your paperwork from here on out."

They all cocked their heads at me like I had just proposed something really interesting.

"I know you're gearing up to protect the Earth from a hell-hole," I continued.

"We feel the disturbance," they all said together.

"That's good!" I said, my voice a couple octaves too high to give off any sort of authority. "That's good. I'm glad you guys felt the disturbance and took the initiative to go over there and keep it closed. Don't stop doing that. I want you to keep doing that. I'm not going to get in your way anymore. And... I... we... your friends already over there need your help and I want to bring you back."

The gargoyles all settled into their places and their hive mind shut off. One of the gargoyles stepped forward. This wasn't a cute little gargoyle like George, the one who protected the engine room of the Empress Adelaide boat. No, this guy was the size of a mountain gorilla carved out of stone. He had an Asian flair to his features, like maybe he once guarded a Thai temple or something.

"We shall help. Gladly. It is our duty since we were formed from the Earth's crust..."

"Formed from the Earth's crust...?"

"...by the great Makers of the Other Side."

"Oh wait! I just learned about this!" I chirped. Points for me for actually paying attention to what Father Killarney had been blathering on about in the pub. "You've been around since the Great Boundary Divide!"

"We all were," he said, waving his arm towards his friends. "We rested and hid in the stone, until the humans could free our forms and give us back our sacred duty."

"I like sacred duties," I said helpfully.

"She does. She is a great respecter of sacred duty," Killian added.

The gargoyle roared, "SILENCE!"

I took out an imaginary key and locked my lips, letting him know I was a great respecter of quiet time, too.

The gargoyle continued, "Do you know of the hellhole which must be closed?"

"I have *heard* about this hellhole coming that needs to be closed..." I replied. "But I don't *know-it*-know-it..."

He cut me off. "It is opening."

"Well, let me know where to go and I shall make sure to take care of it," I offered. "We all put our heads together and thought maybe around Father' Killarney's church... there seems to be a vortex..."

"There is a window in the basement of the church," the gargoyle stated. "That is the opening to the Dark Dimension."

I couldn't believe it. "Why the hell is there a window in the basement of a church?!"

"Why the hell indeed..." the gargoyle chuckled.

I looked over at Killian. "We climbed all this way up a cliff when this could have been over?" I turned back to the gargoyle. "Why didn't your friends tell me about the window while I was there?! I could have fixed this yesterday!"

"You removed our sentinel before he could share this information," the gargoyle admonished.

"Sentinel?! Wait, that guy up in the eaves?" I said. Damn Frank the Ogre and his choice of job allocation to the darkest pits of the Dark Dimension.

Killian piped up. "If we had been aware, we would have gladly allowed him to maintain his post."

"If we are on Earth, we are always guarding a post," the gargoyle replied, like a cranky schoolteacher dealing with an idiot child.

I held up my hands to stop them both, trying to get this conversation back on track. "So what do I have to do to Windex this evil away?"

"Do not jest, Maggie MacKay."

"Do I look like I'm joking?"

"The window is protected by the mightiest magic, but cracks are appearing. As Father Killarney strengthens the structure of his church, he is weakening the structure of the boundary. Shatter this window, and you break open the hellhole."

"Wait. You're telling me that vampires could just come along with a hammer and bust open a freeway to the Dark Dimension?"

"It must be shattered at the right resonance," said the gargoyle. "Like a singer breaking a glass with their voice."

"So what is capable of striking this resonance?" asked Killian, suddenly looking completely at ease and fascinated, and not at all like he was scared shitless by this crew. He was my hero.

"There is a bell that is said to be able to shatter the boundary, made by a young Chinese World Walker in the Zhou Dynasty."

I suddenly thought back to that bowl and how much those vampires wanted it. Xiaoming had looked at it so lovingly.

The pieces started to get put back together. The vampires thought that maybe they could have unlocked his secrets from that bowl. But since I had destroyed it, they were now looking for bigger fish to fry. Perhaps something else made by this same artist.

"If someone wanted to ring my bell, where, pray tell, might we find it?"

Killian stopped me, motioning to the gargoyles to answer his question first. "This object, it would be protected, as all objects of power must?"

The elf was starting to scare me.

"Killian?" I asked.

I could almost hear the cogs in his head turning. "Remember what you said about the objects of power being stolen from Notre Dame?"

"Yes."

He looked at the gargoyles for confirmation that he was right. "One of those objects was a bell."

"Quasimodo's bell?" I said, aghast. "You're telling me the vampires stole Quasimodo's bell?"

The gargoyle sat down, which seemed like the cue for all the rest of the gargoyles to sit. "The vampires..." he reached up with a hind leg and started scratching his ear. "Forgive me. Creatures of evil cause my hide to itch."

"I feel the same way," I replied.

He sighed as he got the last scratch, and then continued. "The creatures of the Dark stole the bell from Notre Dame, but failed. It is now protected."

"And for whom does the bell now toll?" I asked.

Killian raised his hand. "I believe that might fall into my realm."

I turned to him. "Really? You have this magical bell?"

"No," said Killian. "But I am aware that some of the objects protected by gargoyles over the years have been recovered," he explained. "There was a bell among the objects." He began walking back towards the edge of the cliff with a determination in his stride I usually didn't see in his laidback elf-self. "We must go see if they have it!"

"Who?"

Killian looked at me, a look on his face like he was a bit mystified that I wasn't keeping up with him. "The Dark Elves."

"The Dark Elves?" I groaned. "The assassins of the elfin kingdom have this bell? Great. And how do we get it back? Just show up and say, 'Hey! Do you have something which will shatter the dimensions lying around in your shed and can we borrow it, thanks?'"

"Not in so many words," he said.

"Less words? SHOULD I SAY LESS WORDS?!"

Killian looked at the gargoyles and explained, "It is always like this."

"Strange human to hitch your wagon to."

"There is no hitching of any wagons going on around here, let me tell you," I clarified.

"Maggie, we shall travel into the elfin forest. If we cannot find them, we shall beg audience with the queen. She will aid us," Killian said with finality. "The Dark Elves will be glad to be rid of this weapon."

"Now wait just a minute here, Mister. Can't we just leave the bell where it is and go our merry way? No reason to go dragging it out of an elfin forest where it is safe and sound if we don't need to."

"The only issue with that plan, Maggie," he said, "is that the vampires may attack the Dark Elves and secure the bell, if it is indeed Quasimodo's bell, before we had an opportunity to break it. Much like they did with a certain lion statue."

He had to go and throw that damned lion statue in my face.

I looked over at the great big cliff we were going to have to climbing down and thought of all the joys we had ahead of us. But there were worlds to save. "We'll be back," I said to the gargoyles. "I'm gonna get your work permits in order and handle everything. Don't try to kill us next time." I then turned to Killian with a sigh. "Okay, let's go bust some bells."

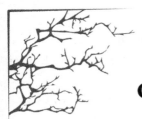

Chapter 20

We got home and I was out before my head hit my pillow. Climbing cliffs and opening illegal portals will do that to a girl. I spent the next morning making phone calls and getting work permits in order for all the cliff-dwelling gargoyles. I was also going to have to figure out how to make a visit to Frank to see about legally clearing the illegal gargoyles already hiding in Father Killarney's shed. As I hung up the phone, I could tell that the clerk was none too pleased to have to deal with the expedited volume of paperwork I was pushing across his desk. I wasn't too pleased with all of the extra fees he kept tacking on. But I guess saving the dimensions from collapse was what savings accounts were for. Once we were done, I might talk to the World Walker union and see about reimbursement. Seems like they should have a contingency fund to cover 'preventing the world's end'.

All that was left was to make sure my pet had something to eat and nothing ate him while I was gone. My normal pet-sitting witch wasn't available. She usually was thrilled to have an extra cat around. But with Solstice just around the corner, she had her coven in for a visit and was overrun with familiars.

So, I was down to my last hope.

"Hey Mom! Can you come over and watch Mac for a couple days?" I said into the phone.

"Whatever for, Maggie?"

"Killian and I are headed off into the elfin forest..."

"Really? You and Killian?" she chirped, suddenly all interested.

"...to track down the Dark Elves and save some worlds."

I heard her sigh. "Again? Really, Maggie. Surely someone else can save the multiverse now and then. I had a really nice dinner planned for the family tonight. What am I going to do with all these leftovers?"

I leaned my forehead against the wall. "I'm afraid Killian and I drew the short straws this round," I said. "But I'll see if I can take a pass next time."

There was the sound of banging cabinets and rattling plates in the background. "It just seems like this is becoming a habit. How many times have you saved the world in just the past few months?"

"Enough times," I said, rubbing my temple. "I have saved it enough times. And not one time too many."

"All this stress is going to give you wrinkles."

"I'll start moisturizing."

"Really, Maggie. This is just too much." There was a pause. "Well, I suppose there is nothing you can do about it. You know, you should see if they are hiring at your sister's office."

"I'll get right on that," I said as I started rummaging through the refrigerator for something to shove in my mouth before I said something I was going to regret.

"So, what are you looking for this time?" she asked. I assumed she wasn't asking about the beverage I found in the back.

"A bell which can crack the dimensions," I said, cracking open the beer... when suddenly there was a crackle on the line. "Mom? Is this line secure?" I asked.

"Of course it is," she replied. "I haven't been married to your father for forty years without learning long ago to upgrade to the secure line package. Really, Maggie."

The crackling became more pronounced, and then there was a click.

"You okay, Mom?" I asked.

"I'm fine. Why? Did you hear something?"

I looked down at the handset. "Yeah. It sounded like some-one was there."

"Maggie, are you saying our line is tapped?" Worry filled her voice.

"I'm sure it was nothing," I replied, trying to pretend like it was nothing.

"What is it, Maggie?"

"It was nothing!"

"I'm a psychic, Maggie."

I breathed. "I just think it would be smart for me to get off the line."

"Well, the damage is done, no need to go..."

"I'll catch up with you when I get back," I said. "I have to run!"

"Don't get yourself hurt," she said into the phone before I could hang up.

"WHAT?! WHY?! Did you see something?" I asked, her words chilling me to the bone.

"I'm just saying you should watch yourself. And stay close to Killian," she replied.

I shook my head, suddenly seeing straight through her devious machinations. "I'll get right on that, Mom." And I hung up. Stay close to Killian... that woman...

Still, strange things were afoot at the Circle MacKay. That vampire had broken into the line the other night and I thought it had been my cell phone. But were they tapping my parents' line? I guess it didn't matter. Like Mom said, the damage had been done. All we could do was expect the worst and play defense.

I loaded up my gear, switched on enough lights in the house to make any cat burglars think I was still around and armed, and headed on out. It was a short drive to the Elfin Forest and, fortunately, there was plenty of unrestricted parking at the curb just for me. Killian was waiting by the big iron gate, standing on one leg like a flamingo. I gave him a little wave before I showed off my mad parallel parking skillz and hopped out.

"All ready?" I asked him as I popped the truck and took out my backpack.

"I am looking forward to spending quality time traipsing through the woods with you, Maggie."

I coughed uncomfortably. "Killian? How mad would you be if we had... company... on this expedition of ours?"

"Depends upon the company. If it is Lacy, I would not be upset in the least."

"It is not Lacy."

"Your mother?" he asked, his tone decidedly different.

"Nooo... not her..."

"Oh no, Maggie," he sighed, reading the look on my face. "Tell me what you have done."

"What if there were some... say... vampires... who might be following us?"

"I would be more inclined to be troubled," he said evenly.

I busied myself with my pack. "What if accidentally *I* was the reason they knew where to go to follow us?"

"I might be inclined to lean less towards troubled and more towards extremely concerned."

"Good. Then let's never speak of this again."

"Maggie..." he warned.

I sighed and looked up at him. "I think my mom's line was tapped."

"And?"

"And when I was telling her I needed someone to come over to take care of Mac, I think they may have heard that you and I were going off to save the world."

"Maggie. Was the line not secure?" he asked me.

"I was pretty darn sure that it was," I replied. "But I am also pretty darn sure from the crackle on the line that somehow they broke through."

Killian rubbed his eyes in defeat. "Then we must exercise caution."

That's what I liked about him. "Thanks for not making me feel bad about this," I said.

He shrugged. "What is a vampire ambush between friends?"

"A typical Tuesday?"

"Very true."

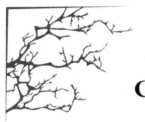

Chapter 21

We stepped into the forest and it was like someone turned off a light switch on all the sound. The street beyond the wall was just gone. Not a single car or carriage or honking cab driver driving a cab full of honking geese.

Just blissful silence.

It made all of the hair on my arms stand on end.

"Little unnerving..." I commented, scanning the horizon for something which may or may not want to eat us.

Killian held up his hand. I turned to see what he was doing. Out of nowhere stepped twelve elfin archers, their bows notched, but not pulled back.

"Oh, so there *was* something out there ready to kill us," I replied.

Killian gave me a "shut up, Maggie" glare and I shut my mouth.

"Killian of Greenwold," one of the elves said. He was an impossibly pretty ginger elf. Long live the redheads.

"Angus of the Glen," Killian replied.

They then just stood there staring at one another. Just staring. Just gazing into one another's eyeballs without blinking. Then, without warning, the elves turned and disappeared behind the trees from whence they came.

"What the fuck just happened?" I asked Killian, grabbing his tunic sleeve.

"I was greeting my friends," said Killian, mystified by my curiosity.

"You didn't say jack shit. You just stood there staring at one other and then they vamoosed."

"We didn't have anything to say," he replied simply as he began to walk.

I jogged to catch up to him. "Wait? Nothing to say? Not even some polite chit-chat? 'Nice weather we're having' or 'killed any vampires lately'?"

"They see me every time I come and go," he shrugged. "After several centuries, you run out of conversation."

"So that's it?" I said. "They're just going to let us come waltzing in?"

"We are allowed to pass," he replied.

"No secret handshake? No password?"

"What do you believe that just was?" he asked, pointing back to where we had just been standing.

"What? The quiet game?" I said. "The quiet game was the secret password?"

"They looked into my heart to see what my intentions were, and seeing that my heart was filled with non-violent intentions, we were safe to pass," he explained simply.

"And if you were feeling violent?"

"They would have killed me."

I let out a low whistle and shook my head. "Remind me not to try to come through when Frank has given us a stack of gargoyle cases."

"My dear Maggie, I believe that you are the one giving us our most recent gargoyle case."

"Well, at least it doesn't involve chiseling anything."

"No, but it does involve tracking down Quasimodo's bell and dealing with the Dark Elves."

"Toe-may-toe... toe-mah-toe... You are welcome to hang from the church rafters all you want, I prefer battling this form of evil. You can't stake gargoyle poop."

"No, Maggie, you cannot."

"Gargoyles are the worst."

"More terrifying than evil," agreed Killian.

I fell into step beside him. "Speaking of terrifying, any idea how we are going to find the Dark Elves?"

Killian sighed as he pushed back a tree branch. "I am afraid that they will make themselves known when they are ready to make themselves known."

"What?! That is an idiotic plan."

"That is the way these things work, nonetheless," he replied. "There is no finding the Dark Elves unless they want to be found."

"That's not true," I pointed out. "Those vampires that stole the statue found them."

"It is the first time such a thing has happened in centuries," he replied.

"Well, how about we aim for a second time?" I suggested.

"Maggie," Killian replied, taking my hands in his. "Enjoy the forest. Revel in the joy of each other's company. We shall arrive when we arrive, and we will rest safe in the knowledge that the journey will be as big a part of this mission as the destination."

"No, I think the destination is actually a whole lot more important than the journey. In fact, we could skip the whole journey and I think the world would be so much happier."

"Do not make me leave you in the forest, Maggie."

"Ugh. Fine."

"Enjoy my home," he replied, spreading his arms wide so that I could take in the splendor.

The elfin forest is a wonderland of beauty: sequoia trees untouched by the paper industry, gigantic ferns the size of VW Bugs, and the wildlife. Oh, the wildlife! Last time I was here, I met a talking fox. Killian was busy chirping out to every deer and bird that crossed our path. And I hated it. Flippin' hated it. I felt I was walking blind. I was completely dependent upon Killian to navigate us. I couldn't tell north from south in this lousy wood. Please note: I'm a goddamned tracker. North and south should have been as easy for me to figure out as right and left. And I was lost here. It set my teeth on edge.

"Any news on the twitter front?" I asked, pointing to a red cardinal who had come over to shout at us a few hours in.

Killian nodded. "The Dark Elves have been on the move," he replied grimly. "This is unexpected and quite out of the ordinary."

"Killian?" I asked, tripping over a root. "If the Dark Elves are the keepers of aaall the great treasures that the asshats of the world can't keep track of, wouldn't that be a pretty big pile to go hauling around the forest?"

"They have several hoards spread out across our forest, and those hoards are each guarded by a dragon or two."

I stopped. "You said nothing about dragons."

"They are very nice dragons," he assured me, coming back to take me by the shoulders and propel me in a forward direction again.

"I do not deal with dragons."

"They are quite pleasant," he reiterated, and then followed up with, "as long as you are not trying to steal anything from them."

"We're not stealing, right?" I clarified. "We're just asking nicely?"

"They usually are quite amenable when asked 'nicely.'"

"USUALLY?"

"Usually."

"Great," I groaned. "Should we have brought them some sort of a housewarming... cavewarming... gift?"

He shook his head at me. "Maggie, you are talking about a being which is even older than us elves. A dragon is going to see through any attempt of bribery."

"Not bribery," I pointed out. "Politeness. You ALWAYS bring a gift to the hostess. You men don't think of these things."

He stopped, reached into his pocket and pulled out a ruby the size of my fist and showed it to me. "Yes, we do."

"Oh," I said, impressed. "That will do."

"Yes," he said. "It will."

"Do you normally carry rubies around in your pocket?" I asked.

"Only when visiting dragons," he replied, continuing on.

"Where did you manage to get your hands on that?" I continued, wondering if maybe he had a few more lying around for a rainy day. I could make it rain.

"It is a family heirloom."

I stopped. "Wait. Killian. You're giving up a family heirloom for some dumb case I dragged you into?"

He didn't look at me when he answered. "Yes, Maggie. I am."

Fuck. "That's really nice of you," I replied lamely.

"I feel that when the fate of three dimensions is at stake, a colored rock is worth giving up." He gave me a sidelong glance. "If it comes down to it, I shall expense it."

"I don't think we have that sort of petty cash lying around," I replied.

"We shall figure out something amenable. After all, you could always... owe me a favor?" He smiled and gave me a wink.

Fucking elf.

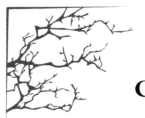

Chapter 22

My head was pounding. We had been traipsed through the woods for hours along trails I couldn't even see. My mind was cloudy. It felt I had woken up with a Nyquil hangover. Killian and I had fallen into silence. He was right that after awhile, you just sort of run out of things to say. I tried to start up a game of slug-bug whenever we saw a beetle, but Killian won too much and I told him I needed to protect my staking arm.

The suns rose up to their highest points and then began their fall back towards the horizon and finally Killian piped up to say, "We should set up camp before darkness."

I swatted away a big spider web and wiped it off my hand on a rock. "Yes!" I replied, dropping my pack, absolutely frickin' thrilled not to be walking anymore. My feet hurt. I smelled. I was completely powerless in this place. I was so done with this entire goddamned elfin nature business.

"Not here, Maggie," he said.

I looked at him. "What? Do you have a campsite close by with cable hook-ups or something?" I seriously did not want to walk one more step further.

"Not here," he reiterated.

I groaned and picked up my pack. "Who cares?! We are in the middle of the flippin' forest. Far as I can tell, we aren't

even on any kind of a path. We've just been marching our way
through random riverbeds and glens for the past eight hours."

Killian led us about fifty-feet away.

"Oh. Good," I said. "This is sooo much better."

"You do not know what creatures will travel down that
path at night," Killian said, putting down his things.

"That was not a path."

"Yes, Maggie, it was."

"Listen, I am a tracker, which means I track things, and
there was no sign of any footsteps or creatures or anything that
would even remotely suggest that this was anything other than
us wandering lost through the woods."

Killian put his hand to my forehead. "Are you feeling well?"

"What?! Of course I am," I said, slapping his hand aside.

"You do not feel the magic?" he replied slowly, peering into
my eyes.

"Uh... did I stutter? There is no magic to be felt."

He shook his head and looked around. "This forest is infused with it. You should be feeling it in every crevice and
nook."

"Well, if it's everywhere," I said, trying not to let him know
I was lying through my teeth, "maybe it is kind of like a nose
which has been worn out. Maybe I'm just overwhelmed with
all of the magic you say is here."

"Perhaps," he said, still looking at me like a doctor trying to
figure out a problem patient.

"Don't look at me like that," I said.

"Like what?"

"You know what I mean."

"I have no idea."

"Don't make me cranky, elf."

"You are already cranky."

"Details, details. Now can we pitch camp before we lose light and find ourselves shit out of luck?"

He opened up his pack and began pulling things out. I started gathering up kindling and wood while he cleared away the rocks and twigs that make sleeping on the ground such a joy. He unrolled our bedrolls while I built us a fire pit. We were a regular June and Ward Cleaver of camping... if June was contemplating ways to off Ward in his sleep for dragging her out to the middle of nowhere.

I looked around our stuff for some matches. "Throw me the fire, would you?" I asked.

He stopped at looked at me funny. "You were to bring the fire."

"No, I said I would bring the fireARMS. You were supposed to bring the fire."

"I did not hear you say that last part."

I put my hands on my hips. "Are you fucking kidding me?! Since when have I ever been responsible for anything other than our weaponry?"

"I thought you were turning over a new leaf, Maggie."

I threw my head back and counted to five. I tried to talk, by my hands wanted to strangle him too much for my mouth to make any words. It was getting fucking cold in this fucking forest and I was stuck out here with this fucking elf until the end of time. I counted to ten this time and tried again. "So can you wiggle your fingers and make us some magic, Killian?"

He gritted his teeth and said, "You know that the only spells elves can use must be prepared ahead of time unless you want to owe me a favor."

"We're not going there! Okay! Okay! We're fine!" I said throwing up my hands and brainstorming. "Flint."

"We do not have flint."

"Rubbing two sticks together."

"Be my guest."

"Harnessing the sun through a magnifying lens."

"The sun is going down, Maggie."

"DON'T POINT OUT THE UNHELPFUL THINGS TO ME, KILLIAN."

He shrugged and sat upon his bedroll. "I do not see what the issue is. I sleep in the woods regularly without a fire. Fire causes the spirits of the forest to fear."

"That's the point!" I said. "We build a fire so the wild animals do not kill us. And so that I can have some hot water for coffee in the morning so I do not kill you!"

"This would not have been an issue if you had thought ahead, Maggie."

"Why am I the one who should have thought ahead?!"

"I am going to need you to stop speaking to me in your outdoor voice."

"WE ARE OUTDOORS!"

"Maggie, you are the one who needs fire and if you expect me to create fire for you..."

"Elf, I am about two minutes away from setting YOU on fire."

He walked over, picked up some bark and a stick, brought it back to me and said, "Be my guest. Perhaps if you learned to rub a stick, Maggie, you could create some heat. It would be good to learn, because it is about to get very, *very* cold."

I snatched it out of his hands and waved it in his face. "Oh! I get it! Is this your big plan, Killian? Let's not bring the matches so that she has to owe me a favor? So that she has to come to me in the middle of the night for warmth?"

"I would not let you in my bedroll if you were the last human woman on earth!"

"I wouldn't climb into your bedroll if you were the only heat source for a million miles and I had been left to die on the arctic tundra by some murderous Eskimos!"

"I do not even know what Eskimos are!"

"They are the native people of the northern reaches of North America and I should have called them the Inuit!"

"Well, I know who the Inuit are!" Killian shouted.

"Well, it sort of loses something when I have to explain it!" I shouted back.

This time, he was the one who threw up his hands and turned away.

I shouted after him as he walked into the forest. "Just you watch me! I am going to make the biggest bonfire and hog all the heat to myself. And then won't you be sorry!"

"SCOOT OVER," I SAID through my cold, blue lips.

Killian flung open the side of his bedroll and I crawled up beside him. Good god, he was like a furnace and I had never felt a more welcome sensation in my life.

"You are freezing," he observed astutely as I shivered.

"No shit."

The making fire with a stick trick was a colossal failure and I guess the only bright spot was he wasn't rubbing it in my face. Finally, he looked a little over his shoulder at me and said, "This was not my plan."

"Never said that it was," I said through chattering teeth.

"You specifically said that it was."

"That was somebody else."

"When you are angry at me in the morning, I want you to remember it was you who forced your way into my bedroll."

"Shut up, elf. It is so fucking cold!"

He scooted over a bit more and I spooned up tighter against him.

"Comfortable?" he asked.

"Quite."

"Are you sure you are not a heat vampire? You are sucking away all the warmth."

"Wouldn't that be something? I picked up some object that slurped up all the heat until we were nothing but popsicles?"

Killian looked at me.

"I did not pick anything up, elf. Turn back the other way."

"Still, it is unseasonably cold." He pointed up at the sky. "No cloud cover. You can see all the stars tonight."

"Oh, you are so not allowed to complain about the cold when you're the one who forgot the matches."

"You said you were bringing fire, Maggie."

"FIREARMS!" I burrowed in closer. The cold was in my bones. I was not going to last if this was what I had to look forward to for the rest of our trip. "Do you think we are getting close?"

"Perhaps. Perhaps not."

"You are a real big help."

"You are the tracker, Maggie."

"There is just so bloomin' much magic blooming around here, I can't feel anything."

"Harmonize with nature, Maggie. Block out the background noise and find your center."

I had it up to my runny nose with his hippy-dippy shit. "All I care about is the center of this bedroll. Scoot. You're hogging the blankets."

He gave me about two inches and for a few blessed moments, we lay there in silence.

"Maggie?" Killian asked.

"Hmmm?"

"Are you asleep?"

"I am talking to you."

Quietly, he apologized. "I am sorry I did not bring the fire."

I rolled my eyes and gave him a hug. "No, I should have brought it."

He patted my arm. "Tomorrow, I shall see if I can find the items I need to create a fire spell."

"Thanks, Killian."

There was this pause, and then he asked, "Do you... enjoy... our partnership?"

I groaned. "If this is some lame ass move to soften me up and then ask if I want to deepen the partnership, the answer is no."

He chuckled, the laugh rumbling in his ribs. "I am serious. Do you enjoy being in partnership with me?"

I couldn't believe we were even having this conversation. He should know this answer already. You don't get over your ghost-phobia and travel through space and time with a person without having them mean a whole lot to you. "Yeah. You're all right. For an elf."

"Good."

"Why?"

"Nothing."

We lay there in silence. This was too weird. I bumped him with my knees. "Not nothing. Spit it out."

I felt him shrug. "It is strange going home, sometimes. It reminds you of the person you used to be and makes you wonder if you are still that man."

"Are you?"

"I do not believe so."

I shifted up onto my elbow. If we were in slumber party mode, I figured I might as well commit to it. "Are you okay with that?"

Killian was silent.

"Hey. Come on. Talk to me," I said.

"It is just..."

He was quiet again. I got a cold feeling in the pit of my stomach and it wasn't the nip in the air around us.

"Are YOU happy to be in partnership, Killian?" I asked.

He was quiet a few minutes more, which really started to get me scared.

He inhaled and then let it out. "I am," he finally replied. "I am. I just sometimes wonder at the life I would have led if I had never left the forest."

"You don't have to stay if you don't want to, Killian," I assured him, trying not to let him know how much I would not be okay if he up and left.

He gave another rueful laugh. "I know. However, we did just have the door lettered."

"I'm serious."

He turned over and looked at me. "I know. I am no longer that man."

I took a second to make sure I meant it before I said it, but I did. "I'd support you if you wanted to go back to being him," I said. I could be a self-centered brat sometimes, but Killian was... well... he *was* my best friend. And I did care about him and his happiness and junk.

He nodded. "Someday I might find myself in the position where I must. But for now, I am glad for this time."

I settled in to him. "Me, too."

We lay there, looking up at the stars and breathing the enormity of the universe.

"Get your hand off my ass, elf."

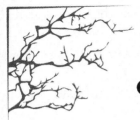

Chapter 23

We packed up the next morning and headed out into the woods. True to Killian's promise, he gathered up all the stuff needed for a fire spell and I, fulfilling my part of the bargain, did not die. So there were two items for the "plus" column of this trip.

There wasn't a whole lot more, though. Overgrown undergrowth, the lack of anything resembling a path, I would have been completely lost if it wasn't for Killian. It seemed like the suns kept shifting their position in the sky, rising in the wrong direction, and setting where they rose. Landmarks felt like they grew legs and moved.

I happened to mention this to Killian and he looked at me like I was crazy.

"Of course the landmarks move," he said. "How else do you think we are able to protect ourselves from an invading enemy?"

Well, color me corrected.

We didn't see hide nor hair of the Dark Elves, but right around Day 4, when we should have been arriving to meet our friendly, neighborhood dragon, we learned why.

The front of the cave was scorched by fire. The bodies of the Dark Elves lay strewn around the ground. It was a slaughter.

The kind of massacre that would make even the most hardened cop lose his lunch.

"Is this where the bell was kept?" I asked Killian, swallowing down the bile in my throat.

He nodded seriously. "It most likely would have been in this store."

A shadow slunk past the trees, almost imperceptible, but my vampire sonar was ramped up like a bat looking for mosquitoes.

"There," I whispered to Killian. "See that one?"

He nodded and pulled back his arrow. Silently, he let it fly. It was followed by the sound of a *thwack* as it hit home. The body fell to the ground without a cry.

"What are they doing so deep in the forest?" Killian mused.

"Looking for us?"

"That was a hypothetical question, Maggie."

"Talking to yourself is the mark of a crazy person."

"I believe taking you through the elfin forest is the mark of a crazy person," he corrected.

"Touché."

We crept forward to the body. The vampire's eyes were wide open. We got him before he could even blink. I'm sure he would have been glad to know that when he died, he was still as pretty as picture. In fact, he was pretty as a black-and-white 1970's Hollywood picture. I'm sure I saw this guy on the silver screen. The plot had something to do with outrunning the law in a pick-up truck. Guess he should have brought his pick-up truck. Still, his face told me a lot. I guess if you've already traded your soul to the film industry, trading your soul for immortality seems less expensive than plastic surgery.

"He is young," Killian pointed out.

"He's a decoy," I said, suddenly sensing that this ex-actor had brought an ensemble cast along for this dance number.

We were surrounded. Vampires descended all around us.

"You did not see this coming, Maggie?" asked Killian, circling behind me so that we were back-to-back.

"Decided our evening needed a little punching," I replied with bravado, trying not to let Killian know I hadn't heard the vampires sneak up on us at all.

"You are a terrible liar."

He knew me too well.

There were a good forty of the vamps dropping out of the branches of the trees like rotten fruit. Guess it was up to us to pick them off. Killian nailed a few with his bow and their bodies fell to the forest floor. Party on.

But the remaining guys surrounded us in a circle, hissing and testing the reach of our weapons. I'm not quite sure why they decided to let us get a good look at them rather than use the element of surprise, but they all were really young with really pretty faces. Too bad I was going to have to rearrange their noses.

"Maggie MacKay?" one of them screeched.

Killian discarded his bow and now his staff was out with the pointy ends at the ready for anyone who decided they didn't have enough holes in their body.

"Who wants to know?" I asked.

The vampires continued circling, and then suddenly the bodies of the guys Killian had dropped from the trees stood up.

"Oh fuck," I said.

Killian had gotten them through the heart. I know he did. That guy could drop an eagle through the eye from a mile away. Besides, his fletched arrows were sticking out of their hearts as they stood back up.

Which meant that we were dealing with Vaclav's cronies: the werepires. Those bastards of a perfect unholy love match that even eHarmony couldn't have lined up. My old landlord managed to get the vampires to bite some werewolves and some werewolves to bite some vampires, and now both of them could only be killed by silver straight through the heart.

I threw my stake into my other hand, drew my gun, and fired a silver bullet, splintering Killian's arrow as it burrowed home. The dead guy dropped again.

Yep. We had werepires.

"Switch to silver, Killian," I said, firing my gun again.

It was just the cue they were looking for, because they rushed us like a pack of angry dogs, which made sense since they actually were part dog now. I wondered if Vaclav had any inkling how fantastically well everything had turned out for him with this bastardization.

With my left hand, I was firing every which way but loose, and with my right, staking anything that within stabbing range. I felt fangs hit my neck guard. Their nails slammed against my Kevlar vest as they tried to rip out my heart from my chest. Their buffeting punches tried to take me down.

And then suddenly, they were gone. Poof. Vanished. Like they had never even been there.

I was lying on the ground, breathing hard. My body ached, but it was a good ache. It meant that I was still alive. I looked over at Killian. He was still on his feet, his pointy staff still in his hand, his chest heaving as he wiped vampire slime off his cheek with the back of his hand.

"Are you injured?" he asked me.

"Nope," I replied, rolling over onto my side to stumble to my feet, then deciding that I actually preferred it here on the ground for a little while longer. "Where'd they all go?" I asked.

"They were moving the bell," replied Killian. "I saw it pass, and they departed to protect it."

"Fuck," I said, groaning. "Do we go get it?"

"We are outnumbered," said Killian. He pointed at the bodies of all the Dark Elves. "They will kill us as quickly as they killed my brothers if we pursue."

The vacant stare of a Dark Elf was looking at me. Too bad his body was twenty feet away.

"Fuck," I said, rolling to my feet. "The Dark Elves didn't even have a chance. They didn't know these weren't just vampires. They didn't know how to defeat them."

Killian reached over and borrowed my silver stake. I was happy to give it to him. He was very quiet as he walked through the slaughter of his people. One by one, he took the end of the stake and pierced each elf through the heart and murmured, "Rest in peace."

I let him take all the time he needed to complete this solemn duty. If vampires could turn werewolves into their kind, they sure as heck could turn an elf. And the worlds did not need a pointy eared, intelligent, undead, ninja-like warrior on their hands.

When he finally finished, he came and stood next to me. I took the stake from his hand gently and wiped the gore off for him.

"You cool?" I asked as I holstered it.

He nodded. "This was a great blow. There are not many Dark Elves left since the slaughter over the jade lion. And now there are even fewer."

I looked at their strewn carcasses. "It is like Vaclav keeps picking targets he knows will pull them out of hiding."

Killian looked at me, startled. "Say that once more, Maggie."

I motioned to all of the bodies of his comrades. "You know, and I know, that these elves are impossible to find unless they want themselves to be found. They have mad skills. And yet, there have been two separate attacks over the past couple months which have resulted in their massacre."

Killian seemed like someone had knocked him over the head with a 2x4. "Maggie, we must get to the Queen!" he said, rushing towards the edge of the clearing.

"Um... sure," I replied. "I mean, we were just going to pick up a bell that would save all of creation, but we can turn around and go visit your queen if that's what you really want to do."

He shook his head. "No. NO! Do you not understand?" There was madness in his eyes. "This! Maggie! All of this! YOU! Do you not understand?"

"Not particularly..." I replied.

He ran back and grabbed both my hands. "The Queen sent me on my original mission to seek out your aid in stopping the vampires from tearing down the Boundary." I still wasn't getting it. He shook my hands as if he could shake some sense into me. "You are the center of all of this!"

"What?" I replied, not liking where this was going at all.

"The statues! The bell! The Empress's combs and necklace! It has all been to draw out the Dark Elves. Vaclav is not trying to just bring down the border. He is trying to wipe out the Kingdom of the Elves." Killian held my hands a breadth apart and moved my fingers so that they were straight. "We have been thinking the vampires are attempting to crossover to Earth to end the human race. But if the Dark Dimension is here," he touched one hand, "and Earth is here," he touched the other, "and the Other Side is in the middle keeping these two dimensions apart," he motioned to the empty space between my hands, "What happens when you apply pressure to both sides?" He took my hands and clapped them together.

The elf was, frighteningly, sort of making some sense.

"You squish everything in the middle flat as a pancake," I replied, locking eyes with him. "And now they have the bell."

"And potentially a dragon," Killian added, pointing towards the cave. "The Queen must know." He picked up his pack and tossed me mine. "We must leave immediately."

I caught my pack mid-air and said, "Well what have you been waiting for? I'm right behind you."

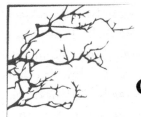

Chapter 24

The elfin capitol is a site that few mortal eyes have ever seen. It is a wonder of tree growth technology that would make a topiary farmer weep.

The elves have this thing with nature. They commune with it and stuff. They ask a tree politely to grow a certain way and the tree is only too happy to oblige. The elves are all, 'Grow in the shape of a staircase' or 'Grow in the shape of a whimsical unicorn topiary', or, in the case of the royal palace, 'Grow in the shape of a royal palace 200-feet off the ground and spanning the width of an entire valley' and the trees are all like, 'Okay' and they grow that way. I'd never seen trees as huge. Fifty elephants standing toe-to-trunk would barely get around the base of their smallest tree. I've seen mountains shorter than them.

I gave a low, impressed whistle. "Wow. How long has this joint been around?"

"Eons," said Killian, maintaining an eerie stoicism. "Before written history."

For the record, the elves have been writing for a very long time. They were doing calculus when humans were still scratching wooly mammoths on the wall like kindergarteners with an art project.

I took a step towards the base of the tree, but Killian didn't follow. I turned around. "You cool?" I asked.

He looked over at me like he had sort of forgotten I was even there. "Yes," he replied. "I am merely gathering my thoughts and examining the best ways to present our hypothesis to the Queen."

"Hypothesis, nothing," I said. "Just tell her straight up what is going on."

"I do not believe, Maggie, that she has ever had anyone deliver news to her 'straight up'. This is important information which must be delicately delivered."

"She is the queen of the entire elfin race," I pointed out. "I think she can handle it."

"Maggie," Killian replied with an exhausted sigh. "Her entire squad of expertly trained assassins has been destroyed by a hybrid breed of vampires. This entire scenario suggests a much greater mind than just Vaclav—"

"You must admit Vaclav is pretty sharp," I pointed out. "And vengeful and cranky."

"Be that as it may, it seems that there is a much larger design to these attacks than we are aware of and I..." He shook his head, like he was holding this conversation more with himself than with me. Whatever he was wrestling with, he seemed to come to some sort of a decision. He nodded his head resolutely. "She will listen. We will make her listen."

We began walking up the steps at the base of the tree. A couple of archers kept us in their sights. It made my fingers itchy to point something back at them, but I behaved myself. I knew they were just doing their job. Still, it was creepy as all get-out.

"Do you think that they could lower their bows just a little bit?" I asked.

"No," replied Killian.

Well, that settled that.

Right around stair number one-thousand-twelve hundred-and-fifty-five, I paused for just a second to catch my breath. "Jeez, how much longer?"

Killian looked thoroughly frustrated that I wasn't taking these steps two at a time. He pointed up. I was guessing we had a couple thousand more. I could feel a stitch in my side coming on.

"Are you kidding me? Don't you have an elevator?"

"We do," he replied. "But it is for our aged and infirmed. Are you aged or infirmed, Maggie?"

"God, you've been hanging out with Xiaoming too much. Remind me to take him off your speed-dial."

A elfin child scampered up the steps past us like he was running down a hill.

"Careful!" I shouted after him. "You don't want to make your guests feel bad about themselves."

Killian sat beside me. "Are you prepared to go on now?"

"NO," I replied, bending over to stretch out my back. "How in god's green goodness can you even think about going on?"

"Perhaps because the fate of my entire people relies upon my scaling the steps without delay."

I stood back up and groaned. "Fine. FINE! Let's go. Jeez, you don't pull any punches do you, partner..."

"Not when genocide is looming upon the horizon."

"Once again, Killian," I said, quickening my pace, "you've got a real way with words."

"You see now why I have been composing my thoughts for when we finally see the Queen."

"Don't you worry," I replied. "You've got the passive-aggressive racket down to a science. You should give lessons to my mom."

"Where do you think I acquired this skill?"

"You're an A+ student. And I'm not even grading on a curve." Another giggling elfin kid came running by me, pretending like climbing these stairs was more fun than a slip-and-slide. "Would you tell them to quit making this look easy!" I said.

"I climb these steps every evening, Maggie," Killian said. "Perhaps if you chose to come home with me, you would not be having such difficulty."

"Are you hitting on me, elf, while I am dying on these steps?"

"I thought perhaps a little distraction might be welcome."

I gave him a friendly push. He grabbed my hand and hauled me up behind him.

We finally reached the top of those goddamned stairs. I gotta say, if it wasn't for the fact you wanted to die, the view was absolutely flippin' spectacular. The trees had grown together to create pathways and stairs up to homes and buildings. Bustling life buzzed all around us with elfin people laughing and whispering soft words to one another. Nobody was crying. Nobody was shouting. It was like one of those utopian love planets where sci-fi shows always end up taking their crew.

Added to that was the fact it was almost the Solstice, so the entire forest was decked out with ribbons flowing from branches and shimmering sun-catchers hanging in the trees. Crystal prisms twinkled from below the green leaves, shooting rainbows into every corner. There were booths everywhere selling traditional Solstice presents. Sun-shaped cookies and picnic baskets, presents and toys. Everyone was dressed in their holiday best, a veritable riot of color. Most of the time, elves stick to something which camouflages them into the forest, but this time of year, it was an all-out spectacular.

Killian didn't stop to buy any souvenirs, though. He bee-lined straight towards another staircase.

I groaned. "More stairs?"

"Yes, Maggie," he said. "More stairs. We must make our way to the petition room." He pointed up to the tippy-top building in the top of the trees.

Twelve years later, we finally arrived. I was crawling up the last steps. I lay my cheek against the warm wood of the floor.

The entrance to the petition hall was a swooping mass of braided tree branches, woven in and out to create the walls. Some of the branches were even shaped to form pictures like some sort of living wooden mural.

The elves here spoke in hushed tones. They wore the robes and funny hats of Those That Are Important. And all of the ambassador fancy-pants elves were looking at me like I was something that crawled out of the sewer. Have I mentioned that elves are some of the biggest snobs in the Other Side? Just because your people have a library containing the history of all of creation since humanity climbed out of the ooze somehow gives them the right to look down upon someone who can't climb up the steps.

Killian crouched down next to me. "Come along, Maggie. It is time to see the Queen."

"Can't she come out here?" I asked, really liking the way that the floor felt beneath my body.

"No," he replied. He took my elbow and helped me to my feet. "She cannot."

"If it wasn't for this whole save-the-multiverse thing, Killian, I would have ditched you at the first landing."

"I appreciate your sacrifice," he replied, walking me towards the doors of the petition room.

The doors opened in front of us as if by magic. Probably by magic, as a matter of fact. If my senses weren't so overwhelmed, I'm sure I would have gotten a little tingle.

We walked into the petition room. The ceiling soared above us. There weren't really walls or windows, per say. There were just open beams separating us from the other parts of this fancy treehouse. You could look out the sides and down upon the multiple levels of the forest below.

Sitting in a chair at the far end of the room was the Queen. I had only seen her once before in my life. Her blonde hair hung in a braid over her shoulder, a circlet of silver sat lightly upon her head. She was dressed in a long dress of blue and silver. But most of all, she had that same strange eerie quality of power. Power in spades. She could probably melt people's brains with a glare better than if she had rays shooting out of her eyeballs. I would have been more intimidated, but I had faced down a gaggle of gargoyles, and that kind of puts things in perspective.

Killian dropped to one knee. I awkwardly sort of curtsied. Killian grabbed my hand and pulled me down onto my knee next to him.

"My queen," began Killian, keeping his gaze on the ground. "We come to you on a matter of great import."

She waved her hand and said, "Speak, Killian of Green-wold."

"Death has touched the heart of our forest."

The queen sat forward. Her pale face seemed paler. "Go on."

"A crossbreed of vampires who also hold the power of the werewolf kind have attacked the Dark Elves. I found no survivors."

The queen seemed to collapse for just a moment before she regained her composure. "All of them?"

"Indeed, my liege," replied Killian.

"And what caused them to attack my people?" she asked, looking for the first time at me. I could feel her loathing, like she was blaming me for everything that happened.

"They sought the bell of Notre Dame," replied Killian.

She stood and strode across the polished floor of her throne room angrily. "They should not have even been able to enter our forest. The Dark Elves should have been able to prevent them."

I raised my finger for permission to speak. Killian looked at me like I better not screw this up. Ye of little faith. The queen nodded at me to go ahead.

"Remember how you originally sent Killian out to see me about someone trying to bring down the wall between the Earth and the Other Side?" I asked.

She nodded at me. "I assure you my memory is quite good."

Great. I had a live one. "Well," I continued, trying to mind my manners, "This bell can cause a crack in the dimensions..."

She stared Killian down. "Why have you failed to stop the vampires from this task? You should have—"

No one picks on my partner. No one but me. I cut her off. "That's well and good about the should haves and shouldn't haves, lady..."

Killian elbowed me in the ribs to remind me to be respectful. I gave him a glare. She was his queen, not mine. But I'd make an effort. I took a deep breath. "What I'm trying to say is that I've learned there is not a whole lot to be gained by crying over spilled milk. The vampires have the bell. And this bell, as I'm sure you are aware since your brain remembers everything, opens up a hellhole from the Dark Dimension straight to Earth, so that they can bring over all their cronies."

"I care not for what dimensions the vampires open on Earth. My duty is to my people and this dimension," she replied. "Why have they killed my people when your race should have been the one to bear the brunt of their schemes?"

"Weeeeelll, there's the problem," I informed her. "Killian and me..."

"Killian and I," Killian corrected under his breath.

"Killian and *I* think they are going to try and mount an attack on the elfin kingdom from both sides. Each object they have tried to gather has resulted in the death of the Dark Elves. We believe the vampires are trying to weaken you."

The queen sat down, her blue gown swirling around her feet. Even on the brink of destruction, she looked prettier than I did on a good day. She was silent for a moment before stating impassively, "I shall have to give this matter thoughtful consideration."

This time Killian spoke up. "My queen, time is not our friend. I ask you, humbly, to take action."

She stopped him. "Killian of Greenwold, I must consider all aspects of this campaign. I must test the truth and voracity of your claim. I must consider which course will cause the least harm to our people."

I again raised my hand with a suggestion. She gave me another look and it wasn't of the warm and friendly variety.

"We know where they are coming through," I said. "There is a portal to the Dark Dimension under a church... there's a window... We have this friend named Father Killarney and beneath his church..." I was getting off track. I stopped myself. "I am here to help and you won't even have to leave the throne room. I'll seal this portal and the problem will be over. We just came here to let you know your kingdom was possibly in danger and maybe you might want to look to that."

She shook her head sadly. "Foolish human, if this bell can do what you say it can, it will break through any seal which you are capable of creating," she informed me stoically.

"Listen, I might be human, but I'm also a World Walker..."

"This is far beyond the abilities of your kind."

"Well, any idea what I *can* use to create a seal they can't break through? I'm open to suggestions."

Her eyes were clouded with thought, but finally she spoke. "There is a way..."

"Fantastic!" I said. "Point us the direction you want us to go and we are so completely on it."

Killian looked like he wanted to die.

She leaned forward, her hands gripping the carved arms of her throne. "You say this window is in the basement of a church?"

"Yes, Father Killarney's church. We are on top of it. There are some gargoyles—"

She cut me off. "The window must be replaced by something stronger, a keystone placed within it which can withstand the piercing."

"Awesome!" I said. "Steel? Rock? You name it, I will pile it in front of the window."

"A dragon's heartstone."

I gulped. "A dragon's heartstone?"

"It is the only thing strong enough to withstand the onslaught."

"You sure that's the *only* thing strong enough?" I asked. "I could get some diamonds or something..."

The queen shook her head. "It is the only way."

So, here's the quick and dirty history of dragons. You've got two major types flying around. You've got the ones that Earth folks associate with the East: the wise and kind ones. The good guys. The philosophers.

But then along came the vampires.

As we learned in an educational hands-on werepire/vamp-wolf demonstration, they can turn other creatures. And when you turn a dragon, you get a fire breathing monster whose can only be killed by stabbing it through the heart via a single chink in its armor. When it is turned into a fire breathing, people eating monster, its blood coagulates and the last drop of their mortal blood turns into a rock called a heartstone. And, unfortunately, the only way to get that heartstone is to reach into their heart and get it.

Which really, really sucks.

"You wouldn't happen to have one of those lying around, would you?" I asked hopefully.

Her face was as cold as the stone she was suggesting we head out for. "I am afraid not," she said as she fixed her gaze upon Killian. "But we do have a dragon."

"My queen!" exclaimed Killian, stepping forward.

She held up her hand and silenced him. He fell down to one knee, again, and bowed his head.

"Wait, I thought you were friends with dragons," I said. "And now you want me to go killing one?"

"If the Dark Elves have been killed by vampires, our dragon has been turned," she replied quietly.

Killian's mouth opened and shut several time as he tried to come up with something to say. He finally decided to just shut it and lower his eyes to the floor. Seemed to be his favorite response to this chick. Just nod his head and grovel.

"Don't you have someone else who can do this...?" I asked, really wishing I had listened to that vampire on the phone all those days ago when he told me not to take the dumb job that started this domino of suck.

"Only one," she said, looking at Killian strangely. "The heartstone will seal the portal forever," she assured, turning back to me. "And removing the threat of this turned dragon will save my people, to which I will owe you a debt of gratitude." She leaned forward. "I shall owe *you* a 'favor.'"

Now, it is not every day that you can get the queen of the elves to owe you a favor. I weighed my options. True, we would have to slay a dragon. But sealing a portal to hell forever was good. Forever meant that I wouldn't have to worry about Dark

Dimensional portals for a really long time. I could handle the headache of this gig if it meant I never had to do it again.

"I shall send you with an army of my people to aid you in this task," she stated, standing as if to call someone from the other room.

Killian cut her off. "They are all dead." The air hung uncomfortably with that little bit of truth. He stood, rising from the floor like some sort of hero in a goddamned epic movie. "I shall see to this matter."

Cue the swelling violins, because the queen involuntarily reached out her hand. "No... not alone..."

Killian locked eyes with her and vowed again, just in case he stuttered the first time, "I shall see to this matter."

He turned on his heel and strode out of the room. I sort of hop-skipped after him, and waited until the doors closed behind us before I grabbed his sleeve and asked, "Are you out of your goddamned mind?! The queen was about to send us out with an army and you turned her down."

He continued on coldly. "There was an army already protecting the bell, and they were killed."

"Still..."

He stopped. "Maggie, there is no help. They are dead. All of them." He looked back at the door. "I should have been here earlier."

"What are you talking about? Earlier to do what? We got here as soon as we figured this thing out."

"Maggie," he replied. "I have slain a dragon before. I come from a long line of slayers."

"Um... how did I not know this about you before?!"

"Why do you think my chosen weapon is a long, pointed staff?"

"You were compensating for something?"

"It is the better to pierce a dragon through the heart." Killian turned towards me and took my hands in his. "I cannot force you to come on this quest with me, but the lives of my people are at stake and I must go. I must do this."

I rolled my eyes. Fucking elf. "Are you kidding me? How many times have you saved my people and not even blinked?" I popped him in the arm. "Don't ever think you have to slay your own dragons, Killian." I looked at all the steps we now had to climb down. "So, let's go kill this muthafucka."

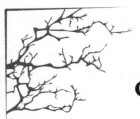

Chapter 25

The bodies of the Dark Elves were gone when we returned to the cave. I don't know if they had some friends who came and picked them up or if the forest was really, really good at decomposition. Whatever the reason, I was glad not to trip over severed limbs. I didn't need any reminder of the fate which lay in store for us if this dragon we were about to face was feeling snacky.

And without the carnage there to spoil the mood, gotta say, the entrance to the Cave of Doom was flipping gorgeous. I mean, I don't even know if you couldn't even call it a cave, more like a subterranean bunker palace. It had big stalactites hanging down like teeth, but the rock itself was veined with gold. And those gold veins, somehow, had been shaped into all sorts of elfin language runes. My guess was via magic, but knowing the way this crazy forest worked, who knew. Maybe it all just grew that way naturally. I gave a low whistle. "Nice digs."

Killian lay down on the ground and I threw myself on my belly beside him, keeping our profile low.

"So, do we just go storming the cave or what?"

He shook his head. "That would not be a good plan."

I rested my chin on my palm. "Well, I'm thinking staying away from the mouth end of the dragon is a good idea."

"I am inclined to agree."

"I hear their tails are pretty wicked, too," I pointed out.

"Yes, that is also true."

"So what we want to do is come at him sideways."

Killian nodded his head from side-to-side in consideration. "Sideways would be good."

"Under would actually be better. It would give us a better shot at the armor weakness."

"We do not have any entrances from below," said Killian.

"Side entrances it is then," I replied. "Happen to have any of those lying about?"

"As a matter of fact," he said, wiggling his body backwards down the hill.

I followed him around the side of the mountain, slipping and sliding along the non-existent rabbit paths that he kept swearing existed.

"You're totally making this up, Killian," I said.

"I assure you that this is a well-worn trail traveled by my people for centuries."

"Seems to me a once-worn trail they *haven't* traveled for over a century," I grumbled as a tree root snagged my boot.

"Quiet, Maggie," he said. "You shall wake the dragon."

Eventually, we reached a tree that had tipped over, showing off its root system. Killian took off his pack and opened it. He said, "I was going to give you these for Solstice, but I believe you might have more use for them now."

He handed a wad of something to me. I removed the cloth wrapping and it was a pair of elfin boots! Real elfin boots! Of my very own!

"Jeez, Killian! These are gorgeous!" I said, admiringly. They were pretty coffee-colored suede that laced up to just beneath the knee. "You really shouldn't have!" I continued as I ripped off my old boots and put them next to a tree. Hopefully, we'd come back to retrieve them. If not, well, next to punching, shoe shopping is one of my favorite pastimes. Sure, these didn't have the steel tips of my Doc Martens, but you could walk through a pit of cellophane and no one would hear you coming. This was going to prove to be useful when stalking a dragon. "I feel bad I didn't get you anything," I replied lamely.

"Extract me from this situation alive, and I will consider it one of the greatest Solstice gifts I have ever received," he stated, looking around the ground for something.

"I think I might just be able to fulfill that item from your wish list," I smiled.

Killian gave me a nod, and then without warning, he gave a hop and a little wiggle and the lower half of his body disappeared into the earth.

"Wait! Come back! What the hell do you think you're doing, Killian?" I hissed.

Beneath him was a hole hidden by the root system by the fallen tree. Killian's eyes flickered up at me in exasperation. "Maggie, if you are going to continue questioning my ability to navigate my own forest, you can return to our office."

"My bad!" I said, holding up my hands. "No need to get snippy! I see my partner go feet first beneath a tree and I just want to know who to call when he gets killed for not telling me what the hell is going on."

"It is the side entrance, Maggie," he replied, smashing his boot against something beneath him and falling down a tad more. "It is grown over, but that is the point. So that others are unable to detect it."

"Seeing as how the vampires managed to get in and turn your dragon, I'm thinking it isn't so secret anymore, Killian. Now scoot over and let me go first in case there is something inside that needs staking."

"I am perfectly capable of staking my own monsters," Killian replied.

"Not when the only thing you are armed with is that collapsible staff of yours," I said, taking off my pack and moving him out of the way.

"I will have you know I have several lethal items on my person with which I can kill many manner of creatures," he said, getting in my way.

"Well, you better get 'em out now, Mr. Lethal Items, because I have a feeling you're going to need them soon."

"I see only one person before me I am holding murderous thoughts towards, Maggie, and I believe it is in both our best interest if I am not armed."

We both squished ourselves down the hole, our arms and legs getting tangled up in one another.

"That better be your collapsible staff rubbing up against my leg, elf," I said.

"I assure you that it is something you would not wish to be impaled with, Maggie."

"That doesn't narrow it down."

We squished down together a bit farther.

"You should have let me go first, Maggie."

"What? And let you relive the birth canal experience all on your own? This is a hoot," I grunted.

Our feet dangled off the edge of the tunnel. With one more push, we dropped into the darkness.

Killian reached into his pocket and pulled out one of his glowy spell thingies. The room was illuminated in a wash of green light. It looked like the inside of a ginormous rabbit warren with tree roots hanging from the ceiling.

I brushed the dirt and cobwebs off my pants. "Tell me I don't have spiders in my hair, Killian."

He reached over and grabbed something from my bangs, cupping it and letting it go through the entrance we came through. He straightened his tunic. "No, Maggie, you do not have any spiders on you."

Fan-fucking-tastic. This was just getting better and better. "Thanks, partner."

"Anytime, Maggie," he replied simply as he put his pack back on and lifted his light to examine our surroundings.

There was a waft of hot air from the left tunnel. It smelled like someone forgot to take the turkey out of the oven. I held my fingers to my nose. "Oh man," I said, pointing the direction of the draft. "I think we have to go that way."

"I would be inclined to agree with your deduction, Maggie," said Killian, heading down the tunnel.

"Wait for me, elf!" I said jogging after him.

He stopped. "We cannot fit side-by-side, Maggie. I shall go first."

"You want me to let you get BBQed? Get behind me, elf."

"Age before beauty," he replied.

"You almost won there, Killian," I replied, looking at him out of the side of my eyes. "Rock, paper, scissors?"

He threw out his hand three times and beat me. Fair is fair. I let him take the lead as I kept a look out in the rear. And got myself a good look at Killian's rear.

"We need to get you a longer tunic," I told him.

"And deprive the world of one of nature's natural wonders?" He gave a little waggle.

"Don't make me feed you to the dragon."

Killian stopped and took a wad of something out of his pack. "Fireproof cloak," Killian explained, draping it over his shoulders. It had a hood and was long enough to not only cover his bum, but drag along the ground.

"This is going to make things a whole lot easier!" I replied, pleased, as I swatted at a root hanging in my way.

"I thought it might."

"No chance you packed two?"

"You did not bring one?"

"I brought the fireARMS. Not the fire-PROOF cloaks."

"Left it by the matches, did you?"

"I guess this decides who gets to slay this monster."

"I shall let you borrow it."

"Age before beauty."

He held up his hand. "I shall have to ask you to refrain from your relentless flirting."

"Ha ha," I replied, pushing him in front of me. "How far ahead do you think this dragon is going to be?"

Killian stopped and lifted his nose to the air. "We have some time. You will know when we are close."

The elf was right. We twisted and turned through that labyrinth, sometimes walking, sometimes crawling on our hands and knees. In front of us was a door ripped from its hinges.

"So that is how they came in," said Killian.

Surrounding the door were several vampires missing their heads. Good to know we weren't going to have to make sure we didn't get attacked from behind.

"Booby-trapped door?" I asked.

"Indeed," said Killian. "There are a series of doors, each more deadly than the last."

"Shame they couldn't have been just slightly *more* deadly," I replied, shoving one of the vampire's away with my toe. "Would have been helpful."

"They must have come with an army," remarked Killian as we passed through the door into another tunnel.

The tunnel was getting warmer and the smell of the dragon was getting stronger. Let's just say there's a reason no one makes dragon potpourri for the home. It was a bit like toasted cow patties, ammonia, and burnt microwave popcorn. Except worse. I took off my jacket, tied it around my waist, and pulled my black hair up into a ponytail. "Getting closer are we?" I commented.

"We still have quite a distance ahead of us," said Killian, shining his light in corners to make sure that the vampires didn't leave any guards.

"Shit. It's going to get even hotter than this?" I said, wiping my brow.

"Indeed," he replied, sweat dripping from his curls. "Much hotter."

We reached another door that had been broken into. More bodies lay around. These looked like they had exploded from the inside.

"Your people do not mess around," I said as we walked by.

"No. We do not," said Killian. He stopped. "There should be more wards. There should be more obstacles. Why has our path been so clear?"

"Don't look a gift horse in the teeth, Killian. Other than the stinky sauna action, I'm enjoying this."

"Someone knew what they were doing," he muttered.

"Say that again?" I asked.

"These vampires knew what they were doing," he repeated. "Someone disarmed this tunnel. There should have been far greater casualties."

"Who would do something like that?" I asked.

Killian didn't say anything. He just kept walking, lost in thought. Finally he said, "It had to have been one of my people."

"That's *ridiculous*," I said. "What elf would invite this sort of trouble into the Elfin Woods?"

"Perhaps they did not know the devastation they would be inviting..."

"Or perhaps they knew exactly what sort of devastation. What are politics like with your people?"

"We do not have politics," Killian replied. "We have our queen, a direct descendant of our original king. And we have our council."

"Does she have any kids?" I asked.

"She has not chosen her consort," Killian replied. He got quiet for a moment but then shook off whatever thought he was thinking. "She has many years before she needs to concern herself with such matters."

"What happens if she dies before she gets in the family way?"

"I do not know," said Killian. "It has not happened in our history before."

"Maybe she should speed things up a bit," I replied, kicking another vampire corpse.

"I shall have to speak to her after we slay this dragon," he replied, quickening his pace.

"Right after?" I replied, wiping the corpse goo from my new boots. "Maybe we could go get a slushee or something, instead."

Killian stopped outside another gate filled with dead vampires. Or probably what once were vampires. Now they were just skeletons with nothing but their pointy little fangs there to show us that they once were bitey creatures of the dark. It takes a powerful bit of magic to blast the meat off a vampire and leave nothing but the bleached bones. And yet, somehow, someone had survived to get through and steal the bell.

"Or perhaps right after," I remarked. I heard a distant roar echo down the tunnel. "Doesn't sound like he is so keen on our plan."

Killian held his finger to his mouth to shush me. And with good reason. Dragon eyesight isn't the best. Two bitty beady eyes for one great big massive body. But they make up for it in smell and hearing. I hadn't ever faced a dragon before, but that's what I heard through the grapevine. There's actually a *Dragonslayers Quarterly* that comes out. Usually features some leathery old cuss missing an arm and an eyeball on the cover. I used to really enjoy reading it in middle school.

"Get close to me, Maggie," he said, his senses on high alert.

I was out of my element and figured at least this time he wasn't using the threat of dragon for a lame excuse to cuddle. I stepped right next to him and he pulled me in tight. He then lifted his cloak and wrapped it around us like a fruit bat. I could feel the wave of hot air as it billowed the cloak on one side, then there was another breeze from the other. This continued for a few minutes.

"What's happening?" I whispered.

"He is trying to smell us," Killian replied quietly, scanning the top of his cloak.

"Think he's having any luck?" I asked.

We waited, watching the fabric of the cloak blow with each inhalation and exhalation. Finally, it stopped.

"No," murmured Killian. He waited in stillness for a little while longer. There was another rolling breath that hit us and then went away. *Then* Killian put his cloak down.

"I'm glad you knew he was going to do that," I said, quieter than a mouse.

Killian nodded, his senses still on high alert. "They are intelligent," and then he added, "and unfortunately, this one is awake."

"What do we do?" I asked.

"We wait for him to sleep."

Waiting is not in my repertoire of things I ever Exceeded Expectations in. In fact, next to crochet, I have to say it is on my list of things I really suck at. But sitting quietly in time-out vs. getting BBQed by a large, undead lizard seemed a much better incentive than those dumb gold stars my teachers were always handing out.

We hunkered down together and Killian covered both of us with his cloak. We sat there in the green glow of his elf-light, hoping that someone would come along and sing that dragon a lullaby.

"Bet you're wishing we stuck with those gargoyle cases," I murmured.

Killian smiled. "Perhaps a bit."

"Don't worry, Killian," I said, bracingly. "It'll be fun! I get to mark slaying an evil dragon off my bucket list, you get to add another notch in your staff."

He didn't laugh, though. Instead, he just sat there, and then said out of the blue, "The queen wanted me to be her consort."

"What?" I asked, shifting so that I could get a better look at him.

He nodded, his face looking way more troubled than a guy's face should be when a member of royalty has the hots for him. "I am afraid my love for her was that of a servant to his sovereign, not..." His voice trailed off.

I didn't need him to spell it out for me. I elbowed him in the ribs. "Could never be royal, huh?"

He gave me a sad half smile. "No."

I had no idea why this slaying trip kept turning into a teenybopper sleepover, but here we were. AGAIN. As long as we didn't start braiding each other's hair, I guess I could stand another heart-to-heart talk. "So why didn't you do it?" I asked. "She's rich. She's powerful. You could have reigned over the whole goddamned elfin empire. Sure beats the heck out of a tracking business in a crap part of town."

"No, Maggie, it doesn't."

I could tell that he meant it. "Listen, Killian, you obviously are new to this. As my mom said many a time to me, 'It is just as easy to fall in love with a rich elf as a poor elf.' I mean, in my case, neither choice is particularly appealing, but for you, the queen is what you would call a 'prime catch.'"

"Have you ever had to extricate yourself from a delicate situation, Maggie?"

"Don't know if you've noticed this about me, Killian, but I tend to be the extricator, not the extracatee..."

"I had noticed." He smiled. "My people live for a very long time and I was not ready to be bound to her for centuries," he said, then blithely noted as he stared blankly into the material of the cape. "I originally volunteered to help you with the boundary so that she would not have to be reminded of the one man she could not have."

"Well that's one way of getting rid of an ex," I replied. Now, I'm a little slow on the uptake with mushy stuff, but the hamster finally got on the wheel. "Wait. WAIT! You think that if you hung around and did your manly duties with the baby making and stuff, none of this would have happened?"

He nodded almost imperceptibly. "If I had placed the well-being of my people first and given them an heir..."

I couldn't believe Killian. "Aw, you old lug," I said, giving him a reassuring hug. I held him at bent arm's length and looked him straight in the eyes so that he would know I meant every word. "As much as you might like to think the well-being of the entire multiverse revolves around your ding-a-ling, let me assure you, it is not."

He wrapped himself around me, resting his cheek gratefully upon my head. "I have never been more pleased to hear you insult my manhood, Maggie. Never."

"Aw," I said, grinning. "I'm here for you, Killian. Anytime."

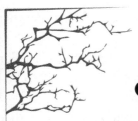

Chapter 26

We didn't say much else to one another, just dozed off and on. We skooched down onto the ground, though, so that there wasn't any risk of nodding off and falling out of the cloak.

But finally, as the little green light that Killian made began to fade, he whispered, "We must go."

I nodded and slowly stood with him. He kept me under the cloak and we shuffled along, hoping the dragon couldn't smell our stinky feet. We passed through several more doors, stepped quietly over a growing number of toasted corpses. Killian waved his hands a couple times in some fancy-dancey magical way to disarm a couple of traps which had reset themselves. The elf had his uses, even if he was a big mushy slumber-party tween of a girlie man-elf on occasion.

We finally reached the door to the dragon's hoard. Or what should have been the door to the dragon's hoard. It had been blasted open from where we were standing and the massive silver and oak doors were hanging from their hinges.

The cavern was lit with fire. There were pools of flame in all the outcroppings and ledges. Guess if you're a dragon, no need to waste any of your treasure on an electric bill. I have no idea what the beast used as ignition fuel. Maybe just heated up the rocks until they were molten pools of magma. It felt like that was the case. Man, it was hot.

I could hear the dragon's breath rattle the air around us. For an undead monster, it was so cute as it slept, purring like a kitten. A scaly kitten the size of a mountain.

This dragon had turned blackish-green, another sign that it had been turned by the vampires. A healthy dragon is red or gold. They get their color from the jewels and flowers they chew on. Kind of like babies who eat too many carrots and turn orange. They'll smelt some gold with their dragon breath and drink it like the latest designer martini. Throw a couple rubies in there and you have yourself one happy dragon. But when they develop a taste for flesh, they start rotting from the inside.

And this guy was the color of a fresh bruise.

He was curled up with his tail wrapped around him on his pile of treasure. I guess it was a bit much to hope he would be sleeping spread eagle like a drunk frat boy, giving us a straight shot at his heart.

Killian signaled that we should take cover behind a heavily carved pillar. I was only too happy to oblige. As we got behind it, it appeared some of the invaders had the same plan on the previous raid. There were the torched bodies of several vampires, as well as a few piles of goo, indicating they brought with them some foot-soldiers. Poor dragon never stood a chance against these numbers.

And unfortunately, Killian opted out of our army.

He motioned for us to take cover behind another pillar, slightly closer. I was cool with that and we ran forward again. He motioned to a third hideout, and that was when our luck ran out, because the vampires left a guard.

I guess if you're going to go to all the trouble to turn a dragon, you might as well make sure he doesn't decide to switch allegiances to... say... someone who didn't kill him and bring him back as an undead creature. That or the vampire was left as a snack.

But my guess was guard, because he ran at us like a dragon is the sort of thing that needs protecting. Guess he didn't get the memo that it was the other way around.

But we certainly did. I pulled out a silver knife from my new boot top and threw it by its tip. Wanted to save my silver stake for a fancier occasion. It landed right in the vampire's heart and dropped him, but not before his war cries hit the dragon's ears.

The dragon opened one eye and scanned the room. He took in Killian and me with no more alarm than finding ants at your picnic, then opened his mouth and blasted us with his fire. We ran and dove behind a knocked over pillar. The flame passed right over our heads.

"So hot!" I shouted.

Killian shook his head and kept me shielded by the cloak. "It will hold!"

I looked over at Killian. "Fuck, I don't want to do this."

With one swipe of his tail, the dragon cleared the pillar that we had been hiding behind. He knocked Killian against the wall as part of the rubble. The elf got up, dazed but still on his feet. Barely. My star quarterback was seeing stars. I was wishing I could call a time-out so we could get a medic on the field. His cloak had been pulled off and was lying just feet away from me.

I could see the dragon was thinking about what temperature to set the oven for this afternoon snack. Time to put him on a diet.

I grabbed the cloak and threw it over my shoulders. I ran at the dragon, not even bothering with stealth. I needed to get his attention off Killian. The creature knocked me to one side with his claw.

"Think you powerful enough to stand against an ancient one, creature of soft flesh and softer senses?" the dragon roared before blasting me again.

I hid under the cloak. The vampire corpse beside me got double roasted. In the vampire's hand, though, was a jeweled sword. Perhaps their plan had been to distract the dragon with sparklies and then poke him? The vampires were getting smarter. Figured the sword had a better reach than anything I had going, so I reached out to grab it. I tested the hilt to see if it after all that fire it was going to fuse my flesh, but strangely, it was cool to the touch. I grabbed it.

"That's my plan! How's this for soft flesh" I shouted as I came back at him. My sword bounced harmlessly off of his armor and he brushed me aside again, knocking the wind out of me and tossing the sword out of my hand. So much for that plan.

The dragon just laughed. "You amuse me."

"MAGGIE! The fire protection is fading!" Killian warned.

I looked at him. "You had to say that out loud?"

The dragon heard. He started marching towards me, growling and snapping his jaws. I gave that monster one look and I took off. I could hear him making chase. Or more specifically, I could feel him making chase. The ground beneath me shook and the pillars all around sent dangerous clouds of dust showering upon my head. If the dragon didn't do me in, the cave-in probably would.

I made a wrong turn and ended up in a blind dead end. I turned around and there was the dragon. Slowly, he stalked towards me, growling and laughing.

And then I heard the satisfying sound of slamming metal, and then a thud as that dragon fell right on his nose.

Those vampires weren't as dumb as I thought. Guess they must've gotten a brain transfusion from the werewolves. They had chained the dragon.

The dragon snapped and snarled. He blew his death breath at me, but the fire didn't breach my cloak's protection. He rolled, and only managed to get his legs tangled in the chains. He trussed himself up like a turkey, out of his own doing. He was so enraged, he didn't even notice Killian sneak by on his whisper-soft elfin feet and toss me a REAL sword.

The thing practically hummed. The moment it touched my hand it was like slipping into a warm pair of jeans fresh out of the dryer on a cold day. This sword had my back. I ran forward as the dragon paused in exhaustion. I thrust it through the small plate and felt a satisfying pop as it pierced the dragon's heart.

The dragon began to flail and I ran to try and get out in time. I made a dive for it, but his hand fell upon my leg. I was pinned.

"KILLIAN!" I shouted.

The elf came strolling over as if nothing was going on.

"He's a fire element!" I shouted.

Killian picked up his pace. I felt the dragon's skin start to ignite around me as Killian pulled me out. Killian jumped under the cloak with me, using it almost like an asbestos shield for the two of us. I could feel his heart pounding against my ear as I pressed myself tight against his chest. Slowly, the roar reduced to just the pleasant crackles of a campfire.

I peeked out from underneath the cloak.

"Thanks," I said.

Lying there in the middle of the room was a large stone that was the spitting image of a ruby. Except, it was not a ruby. It was a dragon's heartstone. And the sword I had used was stuck inside of it, just like the one King Arthur had to yank the sword out of. How did you think that sword *really* got into that stone? The Lady of the Lake? Yeah, she killed herself a dragon or two, too.

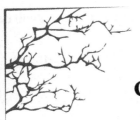

Chapter 27

With the dragon dead, we were able to stroll right out the front door, but not before Killian laid down a few hexes. Never knew when some unfriendlies might show up to lighten the elfin treasure load before the queen could send a crew to move the important stuff.

"So what's the deal with this sword?" I shouted at him as he resealed the backdoor.

"It is something magical," he replied unhelpfully.

"Think I could keep it?" I yelled back.

"I see no reason why the queen would refuse you such a boon for the service you have provided," he said. There was a booming sound as the doors slammed shut and I heard him mumbling in the dark. "Besides," he said, "it is imbedded in the heartstone. I do not see she has much choice."

"If you played this situation right, Killian, I bet she'd grant us a whole lot more."

The mumbling stopped. "Do not make me seal you in this cavern, Maggie."

I smiled. "So, how are we going to get it out of the stone so that I get to add the sword to my armory and we can seal the window?"

"That, I am afraid, I do not know," said Killian, coming back into the room. He was dusting off his hands and wiping his forehead with his arm. "But I am sure that the queen will be happy to aid us when we return."

"Do you think she was hoping I'd feed you to the dragon?" I asked.

"I am quite sure that she was hoping I would feed *you* to the dragon."

"Killian and queeeeenieee... kissing in an elfin tree... k.i.s.s——"

"Should I remind you that there are spiders in that tunnel, Maggie? Spiders I could entomb you with for eternity?"

I backed away. "No need to play dirty, elf."

"I thought it was your favorite way," he replied, with a wink.

"It's only fun and games until someone gets sealed up with a nest of arachnids."

Killian raised a leather-looking thing from the pile of treasure. "I believe this is the sword's scabbard."

"I believe the sword won't fit in there with this great big rock attached to the end."

"We shall have to find some material to wrap it up in, then," he replied, continuing the search.

"We could wrap it in your fire-proof cape..."

He looked like I had just slapped him. "Maggie, that cape was spun at midnight during a blue moon by the highest trained elfin artists... And you suggest wrapping that sword in it? Would you drink beer from a crystal champagne flute?" He held up his hand to stop me before I could even answer. "That is an unfair question."

"Unfair?! They are both chilled, they are both yellow. I don't see what the big deal——"

"Maggie, we shall find something else to wrap the sword in," he said cutting me off in a tone that brooked no argument. "Now, if you will kindly aid me on this search, we can depart and ensure we have the maximum amount of time to save our worlds."

I finally found some green material and held it up for Killian's approval. "Will this do?"

He came over and gave a low whistle, impressed with my find. "Yes, this will do quite nicely. Be sure not to lose it."

"It's some flippin' green velvet," I replied. "If I suddenly find the need to sew a ball gown, I'll tear down some drapes."

"It is armor," he replied, like I was some sort of idiot.

"What?"

"Why do you think I have not died on our adventures, Maggie?" he asked. He poked at his tunic. "Elfin armor. It is as lightweight as fabric, as protective as your Kevlar."

"Are you kidding me?!" I asked. "Why didn't you get me some of this earlier?"

"You seemed so attached to your equipment; I did not wish to insult your choices."

"Insult me! Please! I am *more* than happy to ditch the old for the new! Teach me, oh wise one, the slimming and protective ways of the elves!"

"How much would you like to learn the ways of the elves?" he asked, leaning in.

"Not that bad," I replied, pushing my way past him to the sword so I could wrap it up.

"We are here, by ourselves, in the woods... no one would know..." he said, following me around.

I could tell now he was doing it just to get a rise out of me. "My mother would know."

That shut him up. "Let us head back to the queen's castle, shall we?"

"Wise move, elf."

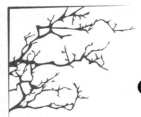

Chapter 28

The elfin capitol was just as we left it, not even aware that we fought a fucking dragon and fucking won. Its denizens just gave us friendly nods of their heads as we came through, like we were normal, run-of-the-mill folks and not the fucking badasses that we were, because come on. We were.

When we came to the base of the tree I put my arm on Killian's and said, "We're using the elevator."

"Maggie, climbing these stairs is good for the soul."

"Killian, I just fought a dragon. I go up the elevator."

He sighed and we walked over to a platform. It sat dangling from a bunch of vines. He and I climbed on, he did a finger-wiggle thing, and the platform began to rise.

The view was astonishing. It is amazing how much more you can see when your lungs aren't dying for oxygen.

But the biggest thing I noticed this time around the capitol was the relative lack of crowds. I mean, not that there were any less people than there were the last time we were here. I just hadn't noticed how few that was.

"Nice that you have some elbow room in this town. I always figured there'd be more of you."

"My people live in balance. We are a long lived and children are rare. Gestation is three years."

"Are you fucking kidding me?!" I asked. "Your women are pregnant for three years?!"

He nodded.

"That's longer than an elephant."

"Hence why we do not have many young," he replied.

"And you lost a bunch of people in the recent raids," I added, realizing the full impact of all those dead Dark Elves.

He nodded again.

"Well, that sucks."

The elevator reached the top and we stepped out.

"See how fortunate you are to have such a rare man such as myself at your side, Maggie? I am a veritable commodity."

"Perhaps I should keep you in your box to maintain your collector's value."

"What use is a toy that is not played with?"

"I've pretty much figured after all our time together, Killian, that you're a look-but-don't-touch kinda guy."

"I assure you that you may play with me any time you wish, Maggie."

"Now, now, Killian," I said, clucking my tongue. "Let's not make your former girlfriend jealous."

"I think it would aid her healing process if she saw that I had moved on."

"Hell hath no fury as a woman scorned," I reminded him. "And since we are going to have to survive the fury of hell pretty soon, I'd rather not level up before necessary."

Killian pushed the door to the throne room open and we strode in. The queen was being shown some sort of scroll thingies by her advisors. As soon as they saw us come in, they backed to the edges of the room, bowing and scraping. Killian fell on one knee and lowered his head. I managed to do a lunge that my aerobics instructor would have been proud of.

"My queen," Killian said. "We have slain the dragon and secured the elfin treasure."

Her eyes lit up. "Did you secure the heartstone?"

"Indeed, my queen," he replied. He turned to me and I pulled out the sword in the heartstone and held it up for her to inspect.

She stood up and walked towards us. She picked up the sword. "The heartstone has been pierced."

I raised my hand. "That was my bad. First time I ever did this dragon slaying thing. Didn't know you had to watch out for the heartstone. Any chance you know how to fix it?"

She shook her head. "Alas, I cannot. Only one who is worthy can pull the sword from the stone."

"I feel like I've heard that before."

"Do not worry, Maggie MacKay and Killian of Greenwold. You have succeeded in your quest." She turned to her advisors. "Go! Take a party of our people to the cavern and move the treasure to the home of the north dragon."

I felt like I needed to speak up. "Are you sure that's such a great idea?" I asked. "The dragon was an epic fail on the security front this time around. And I gotta say, killing that thing was no picnic. It was more of a marshmallow roast, if you get my drift."

I could see she did not.

"There was a lot of fire," I said. "And the only reason we didn't die was because those idiot vampires chained that thing up."

"The vampires will not make the same mistake twice," she reflected, returning to her seat.

"Sorry," I said. "Did you mean they wouldn't attack another dragon hoard again, or just won't bother tying him up. Because both are kind of avoidable if you leave the treasure where it is."

"But you know where the treasure is, Maggie MacKay, and we cannot allow it to stay where an outsider might reveal its location."

What!? I couldn't believe this woman! I had saved the world how many goddamned countless times and she was saying I was the weak link? "Sorry to burst your self-protective bubble, queenie, but I ain't the person you need to be worrying about. You have a leak."

She snapped at Killian sharply. "Explain."

Killian raised his head. "Your majesty, we have reason to believe that that it was one of our own people who betrayed us. As we traveled through the back passageway, the traps had been bypassed. No one but one of our own could have told them how to dismantle the safeguards we placed. I caution you, my queen, to only send your most trusted for this task."

She glanced over at her advisors, her eyes narrowing as she took them in and judged their souls. Man, she was a scary, scary woman when she wanted to be. She meant business.

She turned back to Killian. "I thank you for your words of caution and works of great bravery."

He nodded his head in thanks for her thanks, which just seemed a bit too much on the groveling side for my taste. We slayed one of her dragons before it ate her people. Thanks for nothing.

She continued. "Return to the world of the outsiders and secure the bell. You know where the vampires will be attempting to transport it. You now have the heartstone." She then said softly, "Return to me when you are done to assure me of your safety."

Killian rose, but while he did, I kept my eyes on the queen. There was this wistful look that crossed her face. Man, she still had it bad for him. I hadn't seen anyone that hot to trot since Lacey wondered if they could register at Macys for matching handcuffs. I think the queen was kind of wishing she had never let him team up with me to see the big, wide worlds. Guess hindsight is 20/20, especially when your object of affection has hindquarters like Killian's.

"Come on, buddy," I said, grabbing his arm and steering him quickly towards the door. "Let's get out of dodge. Still have a couple worlds to save before the suns come up tomorrow, including this one."

He nodded and we walked out of the throne room.

I could see why he maybe didn't want to stick around this stuffy place, but wondered when push came to shove, how many times he could turn down his queen, especially if it meant the survival of his kind.

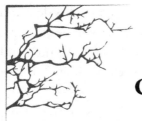

Chapter 29

I drove us through the front gates of the prison, knowing what was in store. The monolith of gray loomed overhead as we entered its maw of metal and stone. It was the home of the most-feared office of all of the Other Side: The Bureau of Record and its administrator from hell, Frank.

"Man, sometimes I just long for the good old days when all I had to do was kill a dragon," I said to Killian.

"Does put it a bit in perspective, does it not, Maggie?"

I pulled the car into a parking space near the door and shook my head. No putting this off. "You coming in or staying out?" I asked him.

"I shall keep the engine of the car running in case we need to make a hasty retreat."

"Smart elf," I said, getting out and closing the door.

I walked up the steps into the Bureau of Records. I could smell Frank's office before I even got in. Whoever decided hiring a one-eyed ogre with a flatulence problem and halitosis for an indoor office was a good idea should have been forced to be Frank's cube-mate.

Guess they figured it was a good way to make sure that all the requests like mine were important. No way would I suffer through this unless absolutely necessary.

Frank was bumbling around behind stacks of paper. The only reason I knew he was there was that from time to time, one of the stacks would sway dangerously. And that he was humming in a low tone. Kind of what you would expect if you ever ran into a rhinoceros with a show tune stuck in his head.

I rang the bell.

Frank came around the corner. He was wearing a stained, white shirt and baggy, plaid pants held up by ratty suspenders. The few hairs he had on his head stuck up with a serious case of bed-head. He rolled his eye when he saw who it was. "Great. What do you want?"

"Frank! My buddy ol' pal!"

"The answer is no, Maggie," he said as he disappeared again.

I rang the bell and this time didn't stop ringing it until he came back and removed the bell from my reach.

"You know all of those gargoyle warrants you've been handing me?" I asked.

"Yeah," he replied with as smirk. He leaned both elbows on the counter and leaned forward. "You want more?"

"Yes," I said, politely. "As a matter of fact, I want all of them."

That made him stop. "All?" He then brought his massive potato-shaped head close to mine. "Why do you want all of them? What are you up to?"

"Just streamlining the process for you, Frank."

I figured that I wouldn't tell him I was going to make sure all of these guys had their permits renewed.

"No," he said. "I think I don't want to give you any of them." He then walked into the back room.

Man, I was a dunce for not figuring out that a little reverse psychology was all it would take to have been free of the gargoyle cases forever. But, unfortunately, I actually needed them. "FRANK!" I shouted back. "I'm the only one willing to take them, so give them to me!"

"NO!" he shouted again.

"Don't let your personal hatred of me color your professional decisions!"

"I hate you on both a personal and professional level!"

"Crankiness has always been the thing I love about you most, Frank!"

"Get out!"

"Not without those cases!"

"OUT!"

"Don't make me call the mayor's office, Frank!"

He came back. "Don't even threaten such things, Maggie."

Here's the thing about Other Side politics. It's not exactly a democratic process. I mean, sure, we have elections. But they are settled on a battleground, winner takes all. Brutal, yes. But this is the Other Side, and if you can't defeat some wimpy mage, how do you expect to control a land being constantly threatened by vampires and werewolves?

So if you are a public servant and accused of nastiness, you don't just get a proverbial slap on the wrist. You get a real slap on the wrist. Usually with something very heavy and spiky. It tends to keep the more unpleasant types in line.

And Frank was pretty darn unpleasant.

He leaned over the counter again and pointed his finger in my face. "Fine, Maggie. You want all the gargoyle cases? I shall give you all the gargoyle cases. I shall give you only gargoyle cases from this point forward for the rest of your life. When you come in here looking for a 'gig', I shall say, 'No' unless I have a gargoyle case."

Great. You try to save the world and end up screwing your professional career. I hope those gargoyles had an inkling of what I was going through for them. I had promised them there would never be an expired gargoyle permit from now until the end of time. I had just written myself out of a job.

But you can't show that sort of regret. Frank would pounce upon my soft underbelly like a hyena. I leaned back over at Frank and gave it back as hard as he was giving it. "Fan-fucking-tastic. You got yourself a deal. Because that is all I want. In fact, if you get any cases requiring a World Walker to save the Other Side? I want you to stick them up your ass and set them on fire. I wouldn't take another case from you if it was filled with requests to bring in pink plastic flamingos from the local craft store."

"FINE!" he roared, grabbing a massive stack and dropping them right in front of me. "Take them! Take all of them! And never darken my door again!"

"FINE!" I shouted back, grabbing the stack and marching out the door, slamming it behind me.

I couldn't help a smile from creeping across my face.

Boy, I loved a good fight.

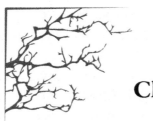

Chapter 30

Killian and I sat in our office, pouring through each of the files and starting the whole process of begging, borrowing, and stealing to try and get these gargoyles the permits they needed to stay on Earth under Father Killarney's care. We needed them. We needed every last one of them. I also placed an order with my favorite online weaponry retailer and bought every silver pointy thing my bank account could afford with rush delivery. Now that we knew Vaclav and his minions were at the center of all this fun, we didn't have room for generic brands. I really hated that this freebie job might end up bankrupting us. But, on the bright side, maybe the world would end and we wouldn't be alive when the ninety-day collection notices started coming in.

From this point forward, I was only taking paid gigs, I promised myself. And maybe I would ask my dad about the career growth potential of a smuggling ring.

Killian finally leaned back, wiping his face with his hand. He looked over at the suns, which were just now starting to think it might be time to set.

"Two days until the Solstice..." he commented.

He might as well have said, "The fog is rolling in and the phone lines are all cut", it was so dramatic.

I went over and flipping on the overhead lights cheerily. "Still plenty of artificial light to burn."

"Perhaps we should call it an evening," said Killian.

I probably should have just left him in the forest and done all this myself. Now that I knew what his daily commute was like, I felt like a jerk.

"Want to come crash at my place?" I asked casually.

His face lit up. "Why, Maggie! What will the neighbors say!"

I rolled my eyes. "I just meant so that you wouldn't have to go loping off into the woods after such a brutal day, only to have to turn around and head back out again."

He gave me a half-lidded smile. "That would be marvelous. I shall look forward to a quiet evening on your couch." He got up and started turning off the office equipment when he stopped, suddenly thoughtful. "The basement apartment here is still empty, is it not?"

He was referring to Mr. Isaac Smith's old digs, the residence of the evil vampire landlord who had been living in the bottom floor of our building all along.

"What brought that to mind?" I asked, wondering if the reason Killian was asking was, in fact, the reason I thought he was asking.

"It would be convenient, and would certainly increase the security of our building, if we had a tenant in that space," he stated.

I gave him a long, sideways glance. "That wouldn't creep you out?" I asked.

"Perhaps not every night," he replied. "But certainly a place to rest on nights like these might be pleasant. You could even join me, if you wished, Maggie."

He gave off just enough glamour to color the picture for me.

"I'll go get the crowbar for the door," I said dryly. I walked into the supply closet and began rummaging through our tool box. "And turn off that glamour before someone's pants catch on fire. They could burn themselves!" I shouted.

I came back into the room. Most of it had dissipated, but Killian totally had some rumpled, sleepy sexiness still going on. I opened up a window and waved some oxygen in the room.

"Glad to know I still have it," he said with a wink.

"Why don't you gas some other ladies, Killian?"

He came over and put me in a headlock, rubbing his knuckles on my head. "Because you shall always be my favorite."

"Come on lover boy," I said as he let me go. "Let's see if we can find you a bed for your nighttime adventures."

We walked down the linoleum backstairs two flights to the basement. The wood paneling gave way to more utilitarian spackle. I flipped the light switch and nada. Guess if you're a vampire, you don't particularly need bulbs to see. Killian ran upstairs and came back with a flashlight and a box of matches.

"Matches?" I asked.

"I shall never be accused of not bringing the fire, again."

"You have a flashlight. We'll be fine."

"It is just in case the batteries die," he replied stoically.

"I just changed them. They aren't going to die."

"We are about to step into an ex-vampire lair," Killian replied. "Have you ever seen a film in which the batteries do not die?"

"That's Hollywood."

"We run parallel to Hollywood," he pointed out.

"Touché. Let's not get eaten," I replied.

Killian and I went down, down, down into the basement. The staircase dead-ended into a really boring wooden door. Up until I found out Mr. Smith was our landlord, I had assumed it was just storage for the green grocer on the street level.

I pounded loudly, just to make sure no one was home. My senses weren't tingling, although dad and I had been here for years and never felt Mr. Smith, so that didn't say a whole lot.

I stuck the crowbar into the door and pried. The door swung open.

I let out a low whistle.

Mr. Smith was a man of refined taste.

Killian shone his flashlight on an onyx candelabra and walked over. "Are you not glad I brought the matches, Maggie?" he said, rubbing it in my face.

"Yeah, yeah. It's very nice. Now get those things lit so we can see what Mr. Smith was up to."

Killian got all six wicks going and then went around to light the rest of the candles in the room.

Mr. Smith had carved out a basement well beyond the walls of the building. In fact, I had a feeling maybe this was dug first and the building was just to disguise the fact it was here.

Killian nodded appreciatively. "Not my choice of style, but it shall perhaps do in a pinch.

The room was filled with purple velvet chairs and red fainting couches. The dark marble floor made for easy mopping. There was sort of a gothic Liberace vibe to the place. Smart of him to go with a color that wouldn't show blood stains in the grout.

In the center of the room was Mr. Smith's coffin, a white box with fancy gold handles. I walked over, unsheathing my stake juuuuust in case, but when I pushed back the lid, there was nothing there but some grave dirt, and the dust seemed to indicate it hadn't been moved since that night in Ghost Town.

"Well," I said. "If you don't mind the lack of windows, this actually is pretty nice."

Killian threw himself down on one of the chairs, his legs akimbo and the ties on his shirt undone to reveal his collar bones.

"Careful, Killian. You don't know what died there."

Killian nodded, running his hand across one of the couches. "I shall have to do some decorating in order to make it habitable, but all-in-all, it has a great deal of possibility."

"Wonder if he left a record behind..." I mused, walking over to an ancient looking cupboard. I opened it up and there were icky magical objects of all sorts in there. Blood magic ain't my thing. "We'll just let the professionals deal with this cupboard, don't you think?"

"We are the professionals, Maggie," Killian informed me.

"I won't tell if you won't tell."

"You have yourself a bargain."

I walked over to another cupboard and opened it. Inside, there were pictures of me lining every inch, with pins and knifes stabbed strategically. "Well, that's not creepy at all," I said.

Killian came over and examined it with me. "He appears to have held some strong feelings for you, Maggie."

"Doesn't everyone?"

"True."

I started riffling through Mr. Smith's papers. "But it's like the old saying goes. Anger will kill you."

"You killed him, Maggie."

"Like the old saying goes, 'Anger will kill you, and so will Maggie MacKay.'"

"I believe I may get that printed up on our next round of business cards."

"It's catchy, huh?" I pulled out a stack of yellowed parchment. "Well, well, well... what do we have here? Record of the statutes... mention of the Empress's set... Oh! And Quasimodo's bell."

"No chance he mentioned any other magical objects they were going to steal in the future?" Killian asked. "It might be helpful. We could get a head start."

"There's a bunch of things," I said. "A chalice... bits of jewelry... maybe we should run this by Dad to see if he stole any of them already." Then I picked up a scrap. "But would you lookie here..."

"What is it?"

"A list of the vampires working for Vaclav," I said. I recognized several of the names, but was a little creeped out how many were new to me. I tapped another column. "But who are these?" I asked.

Killian leaned his muscled chest against my back as he looked over my shoulder. I checked to see if he was laying in some sneak-glamour on me, but nope. It was just him. He reached his hand around and took the list. "Perhaps vampires working for Mr. Smith?" he asked.

"Just odd," I said. "It could be anything from a Solstice card list to the vampire's most wanted. We'll have to check it out. Recognize any of these as the leak in the elfin kingdom?"

He shook his head. "They are not the names of my people."

"Killian," I said, trying to put the pieces together. "It's weird that every time we've faced Vaclav, I've run into someone who said they work for a vampire even bigger and badder than that dude. I thought Mr. Smith was our man, but things haven't really slowed down since he got eaten by all those creatures he created. Do you think there might be a bigger bad out there that we don't know about? Someone Vaclav is fighting against?"

"Please do not even hint that we might be strange bedfellows with Vaclav," said Killian.

"You're right," I said with a sigh. "I guess as long as none of them try to climb into bed with me tonight, I'll let it drop until after we close up that hellhole."

"What was that about needing a bedfellow tonight?" Killian asked, leaning his head against my cheek.

"Don't make me put you in Mr. Smith's coffin."

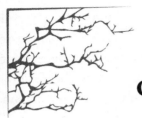

Chapter 31

We slept pretty good over at my house that night. I even let Killian take the guestroom. Since he saved my life a couple times, I figured he had worked his way up from the couch.

That list in Mr. Smith's apartment had me lying awake, though. I wondered how many of those guys were on the Other Side's most wanted list. If I hadn't pissed Frank off so bad, I would see about cross-checking his files. But I preferred to live and it was going to take a couple weeks before Frank would let me darken his door.

The next day was...not tense, but just... well... I guess tense. We had no idea what we were walking into. It could be that our evening would be nothing more than crossing the gargoyles over, sticking the heartstone in the window, and we'd still have time to get home for Jon Stewart. Or it could be a complete clusterfuck and we would walk into a nest of Vaclav's werepires and vampwolves. I had the feeling it was probably a bit more of the latter than the former, because since when did anything go easy in my life. But maybe I'd get lucky tonight. One way or the other, I made sure to have the chocolate cake at lunch.

We made the jump to Hollywood around 3PM to try and beat the rush hour traffic. Nothing sucks more than when you're off trying to save the world and traffic's gummed up by the Hollywood Bowl. The freeway wasn't awful, though, and we moseyed up the 101 until it turned into the Pacific Coast Highway. We reached the Other Side crossover point about two hours later and then were just stuck sitting there somewhere between Ventura and Santa Barbara, waiting for the sun to go down. While the gargoyles are animated any time of the day on the Other Side, the moment we crossed them, the Earth's sun would drop them into stone form and no amount of SPF would stop it until the moon rose again.

And being that Solstice, the longest day of the year, was tomorrow, Killian and I had ourselves a long wait.

As we sat there, watching the surfers catch the waves and avoid getting eaten by the sharks I'm sure were out there, I dialed Father Killarney.

He picked up and I chirped into the phone, "Hey, Father! I have a delivery. You around?"

His Irish lilt came through loud and clear. "Tonight, then, Maggie?"

"If saving the world isn't too inconvenient."

"I have some friends coming over for a card game."

"Fuck. Is Xiaoming going to be there?" I asked, looking over at Killian with a 'well, there goes all the fun' look. He sighed with me.

"Such language, Maggie! May I remind you I am a man of the cloth?"

"A man of the cloth running an illegal poker game in his church. So, is he?"

"Of course," Father Killarney replied.

"Great. Well, the sun doesn't go down until about 10PM, so we should show up around 11:00, midnight-ish. Think your party will have broken up by then?"

"I shall be waiting for you in the rectory!" he replied.

"Awesome. And I'm also bringing over some reinforcements in case this thing doesn't work."

"What thing doesn't work, Maggie?"

I realized we hadn't talked to him since finding out about the hellhole in his basement and the need to plug it up with leftover dragon bits. Seemed like a bit much to spring on a person so I just said, "Oh, just a more permanent solution. Talk about it when we get there."

"Wonderful! I shall see you tonight."

The sun finally set and I opened up the portal just as the last rays were disappearing from the sky.

The gargoyles were waiting.

I held open the door with two hands and the one in the front asked, "Permits all in order?"

"Indeed they are," I grunted. "Rock and roll!"

He gave me a sharp salute before turning around, sticking two clawed fingers in his mouth, and whistling to his buddies that the coast was clear.

The doorway was at once filled with the sound of flapping wings. I hear that down in Texas, there is a cave where you can stand in the entrance as the bats fly out at night. They call it bat bathing. This was a little like that. Except these bats were four to twelve-feet tall, had skin like gravely asphalt dragging past your shoulders, and were utterly terrifying. Other than that, totally the same. I shut my eyes as I felt their leathery wings strike against me and just hoped that it would be over soon. Or the boundary would swallow me whole and I wouldn't have to think about it anymore.

Finally, the last one came through and I fell out of the portal, completely drained.

Gotta say, I was pretty darn grateful for Killian at that moment. His arms were there to catch me before I face-planted into the highway. He threw my arm over his shoulder and wrapped his arm around my waist, helping me to the car.

"Fuck," I said, laughing at how fucking exhausted I was. A monster could come out of the sea right now and I would have stepped gratefully into his jaws. "And the vampires think they can do something like that with a damned bell?"

Killian opened the passenger door to my Civic and helped me in, picking up my feet and swiveling me in my chair. He even reached over to fasten my safety belt, that sweetie. Dying in a car accident was the least of my worries right now.

He swept back my hair. "Are you in need of medical assistance, Maggie?"

"No," I said, waving him off. "Just exhausted..." I could barely keep my eyes open. "Rock and... roll..."

The last thing I really remember before I drifted off was the flock of gargoyles flying like pelicans against the moonlit sky.

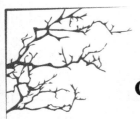

Chapter 32

"You let her WHAT?!" shouted my dad.

I opened my eyes and realized Killian had scooped me out of the car and carried me into my sister's house without me even knowing it.

"Shut up, Dad," I murmured, just wanting the loud voices to stop.

I felt Killian set me down on something soft. I opened my eyes. It was Mindy's couch. I liked Mindy's couch.

"Could I have some pie?" I asked as I drifted in and out.

"She could have been killed holding open a rift that long!" Dad shouted some more.

"I'm fine..." I said sleepily. "I just want some pie."

"That's the very least of what you need right now!" he yelled. "PIPISTRELLE!"

I heard the brownie's little feet come skipping into the room and then a frightened little squeak. "What has happened to Tracker Maggie? Has the elf failed in trying to protect her?"

I skooched into a sitting position, my head throbbing to beat the band. The room was so bright. It was like a bad Cinco de Mayo hangover, and I hadn't even had any tequila. "I'm fine, Pipistrelle. I just need some coffee and lots and lots and lots of sugar."

He scrambled off, wringing his hands, and I heard him banging around the kitchen.

"Maggie, what have I told you about opening up illegal portals by yourself?!" Dad continued to shout.

"Well, you went and got retired, so I had to do it myself," I muttered, every vibration in my head causing the world to pound against my eyes.

"I am right here!" he said. "I would have helped you!"

Pipistrelle came back, balancing a tray of orange juice, Coke, sweet tea, Kool-aid, and Mindy's sugar bowl. "I will get you more!" he promised as he set it down on the coffee table by me."

I waved him off. "This is great, Pipistrelle. It is a smorgasbord of diabetes and exactly what I need right now."

I picked up the Coke, poured some sugar in it, and chugged it down without pausing to breathe. All those keg stands in high school were finally being put to good use. I felt better already.

"Why, pray tell, Maggie, were you holding open the dimensions?" asked Dad, giving me the sixth-degree like he caught me sneaking out of my bedroom window at night.

"Why, pray tell, Killian, did you bring me home instead of to the church?" I asked, giving him the stink-eye.

"You were unconscious and I thought you were dying," replied Killian.

"I wish I was," I replied.

"Answer me!" shouted my dad.

There were too many loud noises in the room. "I had to let a bunch of gargoyles through," I said, picking up the Kool-Aid.

"As one does," Dad replied, making it clear he was expecting a bit more explanation than I was giving.

I flopped back into the couch and closed my eyes, holding the icy glass to my temple. "The vampires are trying to destroy the world again and I need an army."

"Do you have paperwork for those gargoyles?" he asked.

"Jesus, you're starting to sound like Frank."

"And when is this little war that you are embarking on?"

"Tomorrow night."

"Solstice?"

"It's the most beautiful light of the year," I replied holding up my glass as a toast.

Dad threw up his hands and paced Mindy's living room. "That thing could have collapsed on you and you would have been stuck in the boundary forever. Do you understand what that means?"

I looked at him dryly. "Yeah. I have some inkling."

"I don't think you do, because I was stuck in that place for three years and let me tell you, it is no picnic."

"Dad, I just killed a dragon, I'm getting ready to face off against whatever hordes the Dark Dimension can throw at me. Think we could continue this conversation after we get this rift situation settled?"

"YOU KILLED A DRAGON!?" he shouted. He pointed his finger at Killian. "YOU LET HER....?!" He sputtered. "You went off and killed a dragon... WITHOUT ME?!"

He sat down sadly.

Mom walked into the room. "What is with all this shouting?"

Dad looked at Killian and then at me and then said, "Nothing, dear."

"Oh good," she replied, walking into the kitchen. "It's getting late. Shouldn't we go to bed so we can let the kids go home?"

We all let out a collective breath. I had no idea why my mom wasn't losing her mind right, now, but if for some reason she hadn't picked up on it, I wasn't going to alert her to the situation.

Dad got up. "I always wanted to kill a dragon."

"Next time, Dad," I said, patting his arm.

Killian sat down and handed me the glass of orange juice. I dutifully chugged it and wiped my mouth. "Wonder why Mom didn't know what was going on?"

"It is the heartstone," said Killian. He pointed to the sword, which was wrapped up and lying on the coffee table. I don't know how Mindy felt about putting weapons on her Chippendale furniture, but I wasn't going to let her know what was inside the wrapped package.

"Oh!" I said, feeling like an idiot.

Dragons are pretty cool animals, from a magical perspective. Besides being able to eat most creatures in a single gulp, one of the reasons they make such great guardians of treasure is because they can mask magical vibrations. They're like a great big set of noise cancelling headphones.

"Kind of wish we didn't have to go sticking this stone in the window," I said. "Would have been nice to just keep around."

Killian nodded. "Well, perhaps we shall encounter another turned dragon who needs dispatching and acquire an extra."

"I'm gonna pass," I said. I sat up and stretched. I was feeling a whole lot better. Not great, but better. "We should go get this thing done."

He nodded. "Best to do it before hell descends upon us tomorrow."

"We would have gotten it done by now if you hadn't freaked out," I told him as I gathered up the sword.

"Noted. Next time, I shall leave you for dead."

"Thanks."

"A pleasure."

"So, what time is it?"

"We should be able to be at the church before midnight," Killian said, opening the door for me.

I walked outside. "I've always prided myself on my procrastination skills, but this is one time in my life I'm actually kind of proud how on top of our game we are."

I didn't have an inkling how behind the ball we actually were. In fact, we weren't even playing the right game.

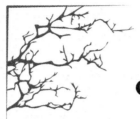

Chapter 33

We pulled into the parking lot. Xiaoming was smoking on the steps of the rectory and Father Killarney was keeping him company. It was the first time I had ever seen Xiaoming out of his bathrobe. He cleaned up well. His hair was slicked over neatly and he was sporting a nice short-sleeved, button-up shirt and khakis. I got out of the car and walked around to the back to grab the sword and my pack. Last thing we needed was some tough breaking into my Honda and stealing the key to saving the world while we were busy getting caught up on the weather.

Although, with Xiaoming around, I knew there would be no polite weather talk.

"Are you coming here to make trouble on the night I was to win back all Father Killarney owes me?" Xiaoming accused.

I looked at Killian. He wasn't getting out of the car. He just stared straight ahead. I was completely on my own. Wuss.

"Yeah, Xiaoming," I said. "That was the plan. Collapse two dimensions to fuck up game night."

Xiaoming pointed his finger at Father Killarney. "I knew it."

"Not really!" I said. "Jesus."

"Maggie, no need for language like that on holy ground."

"I'm standing in a four square court," I replied.

"All the same."

I popped the trunk and swung my pack onto my shoulders. I also pulled out the empty scabbard and strapped it on, thinking it would be nice to have on hand if I managed to get the sword free. Killian finally got out. "About time," I muttered.

"You seemed to have matters well in hand," he replied, giving a friendly smile to the guys.

"Did the gargoyles arrive?" I asked Father Killarney as I ignored my partner, grabbed the wrapped sword, and shut the trunk loudly.

"Indeed! Thank you for the extra protection!" Father Killarney said, pointing towards the roofline.

I looked up at the eaves of the church. What had been a rather plainly decorated church was now groaning with carved-looking statuary. All the eyes of the gargoyles were upon us, their concrete heads turning almost as one to track Killian and my movements. I tried not to shit my pants and gave them an awkward wave. "Evening, fellas! Thanks for coming!"

The largest gargoyle opened up his stony mouth. "Thank you for the work permits."

I looked over at the shed where normally the gargoyles hung out and then squinted into the darkness. "Xiaoming, are those your guardians?"

His lions were flanking the door and swiveled their concrete heads towards me to growl.

"They are lonely when I am gone," he replied.

"Great," I said as I hefted the sword upon my shoulder. "The more the merrier. Let's get going, shall we? Just need to do some repair work down in your basement, Father, and then we'll be on our way."

"I shall get my keys," said Father Killarney. "It should be fine. We had some of our contractors down there doing some work in our chapel room, but I believe as long as we watch where we're going, it should not be too hazardous. They had to cut the power, but I have a flashlight."

I stopped. I put my hand on Killian's arm. I looked at him and our brains were going to the exact same place.

"What?" I asked.

"Oh, we had the new bell installed today," Father Killarney replied, pointing up at the bell tower. "The vibrations from the equipment caused a pipe to leak, and as they went in to repair the pipe, they found an electrical problem. Really, for a building this old, it is to be expected."

Killian and I both looked up at the bell tower.

"Quasimodo's bell," Killian whispered.

"What?" asked Father Killarney curiously.

Oh we were fucked. We were so completely utterly fucked.

"Has that bell rung yet?" I asked.

"No," he replied. We were going to save it for a special blessing on Sunday."

If anyone rang that bell, we were never going to make it to see next Sunday.

"Father, it is really, really important that you do not ring that bell."

"Why is that?" he asked.

"Because if you do, you will open up a hellhole directly beneath your church."

That made Father Killarney and Xiaoming stop.

"It was built by the same guy who built that bowl I showed you, Xiaoming," I explained.

"He built this bell?" Xiaoming restated, just to clarify he heard me right. "This is the dimensional bell of the Zhou Dynasty?"

I nodded. "This church is over a vortex, and the weakest point is in a glass window in your basement, Father Killarney. It just so happens the tone of the bell that your contractors installed today can shatter it."

He might be a cranky old man, but Xiaoming was brilliant in a crisis. He whistled to his concrete lions. "Come!" he shouted.

They came running across the playground and I fought the urge to start running in the other direction.

Xiaoming looked up at the sky and then waved his finger at us. "I will silence the bell. You fix the window." He muttered something in Mandarin as he started walking. He shouted at the eaves. "Why you so lazy? Guard the skies!"

The gargoyles didn't even hesitate. In one movement, they took off like a flock of pigeons. I guess even beings more terrifying than evil were terrified of Xiaoming.

All the lights in the church were out as Father Killarney walked us through. I tried the light switches. They didn't come on.

"They cut the power to the entire building?" I asked Father Killarney.

He shook his head apologetically. "It appears they did."

"It is like they knew we would be coming," Killian thought out loud.

The only light came from the rows of candle offerings sitting in each devotional saint's niche. I gave myself a couple "signs of the cross" as I passed each one. I was going to need all the blessings I could get. We walked onto the altar, around the back, and down some marble steps into the church's crypt.

On an average day, this was actually a lovely, brightly lit catacomb. Sure, there were dead people buried in the walls with slabs of marble marking their final resting spots, but if your idea of an afterlife retreat is shoving your bodily remains in an indoor storage facility rather than being eaten by worms, this was a nice place to choose.

Except, today it was not a lovely, brightly lit catacomb. It was a grave as dark as a grave, so to speak.

"This is ridiculous," I said. "How am I supposed to fight the forces of darkness in the dark?"

"You aren't," said a voice. It grabbed me around the waist and I felt it scrabbling to bite its fangy things into my neck.

Father Killarney's flashlight was knocked onto the ground.

"Get the hell off me!" I shouted. I ripped my stake out of its holster and stabbed the vampire through his ear.

It just slowed him down, but I was in need of that bonus time to either hit him through the heart or set him on fire. While the fire option is way more fun, I figured Father Killarney might not forgive me for ruining the priceless artifacts in his church, and I managed to grope around and find the vampire's sweet spot before he got me with his canines.

I heard Killian struggle. My eyes were starting to adjust. I pulled the sucker off him and got that vampire through the solar plexus.

I heard Father Killarney shouting something in Latin and then heard the sound of sizzling flesh. The vampire attacking him backed right into my stake. I didn't even have to try.

And then all was silent.

"Everyone okay?" I asked.

Father Killarney picked up the flashlight just in time for me to see another sucker sneaking up behind him. I nailed the guy before he could get another step closer. And the five other vampires that followed as they tried to play Seven Minutes in Heaven in this dark little antecloset.

"FUCK," I said as I got the last one. "This is SO. NOT. COOL."

Father Killarney swung the flashlight around, scanning the darkness for anything else that might be there. Killian grimaced, shielding his eyeballs as the light hit him in the face.

Father pointed it down the hallway.

"You'd think you would have some emergency lights down here in case of... you know... an emergency," I muttered at him.

Father Killarney said, "I shall make a change order to our contract."

I looked down at the vampire who had attacked him. There was a burn mark in the perfect shape of a cross right across his forehead.

"Nice one," I complimented.

"He should not have been able to step on hallowed ground," Father Killarney remarked grimly. "Who the feck desecrated my church?"

I have never seen Father Killarney that mad. I put my hand on his forearm to calm him down. "What's more important now is to figure out where they are all coming from so that we can stop it."

Killian took Father Killarney's hand and pointed the flashlight at the wall. The marble stones to the tombs were broken.

Great. Well, there you had it.

I dropped my pack onto the ground and started rifling through it. I made a mental note to invest in some miner's helmets next time I was involved in a surprise raid. I found the flashlights at the bottom of my bag. I tossed one to Killian and tucked another into my belt as I wiped the vampire guts off my stake and out my gun. I tucked the sword into the pack and threw it over my shoulders. Things were gonna get ugly quick and a well-padded package with a stone covering the pointy bit was about as useful as a Nerf gun in a tiger cage.

The hallway wound around the mausoleum, each of the tiles in the walls holding some dude in permanent slumber who could potentially wake up and off us all if we didn't get that artifact in the right hole in time. We were so deep underground, I hoped we'd at least get some warning if the bell began to toll.

"The thing bugging me, Killian, is not knowing how many guards are down here." And like that, another vampire jumped out at me. I staked him. "You know, like that guy."

Killian shone his light on the sucker. "That is a legitimate concern."

"Okay, so we have absolutely no element of surprise, right?"

"I believe we gave that up the moment we walked into their trap."

"Do we have any defensible position?"

Another vampire sprung out of a niche in the wall and I nailed him.

"No."

"Fantastic," I said as I watched the vampire fall to the ground.

"How many vampires do you think could fit down here, Maggie?" Father Killarney asked, raising his crucifix.

"Um... a lot."

"Whining will not make the situation better, Maggie," Father Killarney said, his eyes never stopping as he scanned for any flicker of movement.

"It makes me feel better."

"Count your blessings. There are vampire-deprived trackers in China who would be grateful for this sort of adventure."

A vampire snuck up behind Killian. He dropped his flashlight as he grabbed the vampire by the neck and flipped him over his head. I landed a shoe on the vampire's shoulder and skewered him good. Father Killarney pressed himself against the wall of tombs, crossing himself furiously.

"What were you saying, Father?"

"That I would like to move to China."

We continued down the passage.

"How can there be this many vampires this side of the border? I mean, did we do NOTHING to help matters when we defeated Vaclav?" I asked.

"As you have often said, it is quite easy to travel through the veil to Earth. It is getting back that is the problem," noted Father Killarney.

"At least they are not werepires," said Killian, shining his light on a wall of broken tombs. Boy, that was a lot of reanimated corpses.

"You'd think if you wanted to guard the most precious strategic location in three dimensions, you'd put your toughest guys on the job."

"Perhaps they were not expecting you until the Solstice," said Father Killarney.

"Perhaps this is not Vaclav's doing," said Killian.

The hallway opened up into a vault and the rose window in the nook shone with an eerie light. It was blue and nighttime-ish. The thing was, we were underground and that window, really, was only lit because there was a switch you could flip and it would backlight the thing. Except the electricity was out. So, that meant it was lit by something else. Like, maybe, a rift in the time/space continuum and light from some demon-infested hellish dimension which was seeping through.

There was a plum-sized hole right in the middle of the window that looked like a single piece of stained glass had been knocked out. The blast of energy coming from it was like walking into a stiff wind. It was blowing and blowing hard. The entire place stank of brimstone.

I put my hand up to shield my eyes. "Smell that, Killian?"

"Quite," he replied grimly.

"Has that piece of glass always been missing?" I asked Father Killarney.

"No," he said, angrily. "We had a piece of amber with a saint's holy relics there. What sort of a hoodlum comes into a church to steal a saint's remains?"

A wave of hellfire spewed through the hole like someone turned on a propane torch.

"I think we met a bunch of them there in the hall," I replied. "Which saint was it?" I asked.

"St. Vivian," Father Killarney stated.

"How did she die?"

"Burned at the stake."

"Pity that seems to be happening again," said Killian as another wave of fire came through.

"A martyr's work is never done."

"So I suppose the repair work you were alluding to was replacing this missing piece?" Father Killarney asked.

"Yep." I pulled the sword out of my pack and unrolled it. I took the sword by the hilt and started walking forward, aiming the heartstone for the open gap. It felt almost as if the hell-hole knew we were coming to patch it up. It decided to spit up a bunch of demons at us.

Father Killarney raised his crucifix and held it high as he started praying loud. It created almost this umbrella of protection. I could see the streams of power hurtling towards us, but felt nothing. Not a darn thing, thank god, because all my and Killian's time was spent trying to ward of the demons and muscle our way through to the wall. I heard feet kicking from the inside of the mausoleum niches. We were about to have a much bigger problem on our hands if we didn't get this settled right this very moment.

"Can we move faster?" I asked.

"It is all I can do to move us forward safely step by step."

"Can I just rush it?"

"It would most likely melt your skin off your bones."

"Fantastic," I said, swinging at a demon as he tried to take a swipe at us. Holiness and salt, that's pretty much your only two tools for fighting these sorts of demons. They laugh at silver bullets and stakes. Holy water, fortunately, will burn holes in them like battery acid but the baptismal font was upstairs. Really, the only thing you could do is bind them and wait till morning. We didn't have until morning.

"Can you create a salt circle, Father?" I asked. Whatever he could do to speed up the binding part of this adventure would be a-ok in my book.

"It is very hard to create a salt circle around a window in the wall, Maggie."

"Damn you, gravity!"

"We must just keep moving."

So, that's what we all three did. Heads down. One foot in front of another. Father Killarney muttered, "I'm going to have to come down and reconsecrate this entire place..."

Can't say that I envied the task. He kept muscling forward, probably using his indignation over all the extra work to fuel his fire. If there was one thing he hated, it was metaphysical housework.

Finally, we reached the window. I stretched up with the heartstone and using the sword to maneuver it, got it placed in the center of the glass.

And for about a half a second, it seemed like it worked.

And then the sword maybe decided I was the chosen one, or maybe decided it didn't want to hang out in hell for all eternity, because it slid out of the stone.

And all hell broke loose.

Quite literally.

"What the feck did you do, Maggie?!" shouted Father Killarney.

The heartstone... the hole in the middle. The stone didn't seal up the portal, that damned hole in the middle created the perfect opening to the hellhole using the hardest material in three dimensions to keep it open.

Now I knew why we had been met with just enough resistance to make it seem like they didn't want us to succeed, but not enough to actually stop us. It was a trap. It was all a trap to get us here. How did they know that the heartstone we carried had been pierced by a sword? I tried to shove the heartstone through by banging the hilt of the sword on it, but it was sealed in place.

The ground beneath us began to vibrate. I backed away, sword in hand.

"Run," I said, and then shouted. "RUN!"

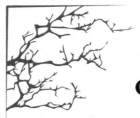

Chapter 34

We ran out of there like the hounds of hell were nipping at our heels. Because they were. We poured out of the church and I shouted to the skies. "INCOMING!"

But the gargoyles were engaged in their own mess. The skies were filled with gargoyles and demons and vampires, biting and tearing into one another.

"There is no way this isn't getting on the six o'clock news," I groaned. I was totally going to have my tracking license pulled. You know. If we survived.

Xiaoming came running towards us and his lions took down the beasts behind us. He looked like shit. His neat hair was mussed; his shirt was dripping with sweat. He wiped his face on his sleeve.

"How'd it go, Xiaoming?" I asked. "Any luck breaking the bell."

"No," he said. "There is big trouble."

He pointed up. The night lit up as bright as day as a plume of fire streaked across the sky.

Dragons. Thar be dragons.

A great big purple one.

The gargoyles were on him, dashing themselves against his hide. But he was so tough, they were only breaking their teeth. He'd give a flick of his tail and the gargoyles went spinning, some of them crashing into the side of the building and shattering into rubble and dust.

We stood there as he threw a gargoyle into the side of the bell. The bell didn't fully ring, but it was enough.

I pointed up at the sky, at the fissure that had spread through the air. "You see that?"

Killian nodded. "One would have to be blind not to."

"Oh, the tin tinabulation of the fucking bells, bells, bells..." I muttered wondering what the hell to do.

"To what you're referring?" asked Killian.

"American poet named Poe. You'd like him." I looked at him. "Actually, you probably wouldn't."

Another gargoyle struck the bell, hurtled towards it by the dragon. I pointed at the tower. "If they break the bell as it is ringing, that window becomes a permanent portal between here and the Dark Dimension."

The dragon spewed fire. The gargoyles continued to dart at him and he opened up his mouth and crunched down on one. Didn't slow him down one bit.

"We are so toast. If we could just get to the bell tower..." An idea formed in my mind. I turned to Killian. "Killian, I need you to distract that dragon."

He looked at me like he was waiting for me to say 'just kidding'. No such luck.

"I mean it, Killian. I need to figure out a way to muffle that bell."

He pointed up at it. "How much needs to be silenced?"

"Xiaoming?" I asked.

"Enough so the sound cannot be heard by the window," he replied.

Killian snapped his fingers. "I have it. Maggie, *you* distract the dragon. I have your muffle."

"That was not the plan!"

He took off at a flat sprint.

"Where are you going?" I called after him.

"I shall return!" he called back.

I turned and looked up that that dragon. He was setting fire to the strip-mall next door. Copy shops and overpriced hipster frozen yogurt spots were going up in flames. Made you think maybe the dragon wasn't all evil.

But that sort of reflection wasn't what I was here to do.

"Go make sure nothing comes out of the church to sneak up on me," I said to Father Killarney and Xiaoming as sheathed my sword, cracked my neck, and pulled out my gun. "I need some elbow room."

They didn't need me to ask them twice. They raced towards the church, bringing Xiaoming's lions with them. When they were safely out of the way, I took aim and fired off a shot at the dragon's eye.

Naturally, if you shoot something at a creature's eye, they can see it coming, and in the case of a dragon, get out of the way. But my goal wasn't to kill him, it was to get him to think about something other than whatever mission he had planned in that walnut brain of his.

He turned in the air and came straight at me, fire burning up everything in his path. I ducked behind the corner of the stucco shed. It wasn't a ton of protection, but it gave me a little shield.

I could hear him flapping his great big wings overhead looking for me. The earth shook as his feet hit the ground. I could hear the sound of his claws scraping the concrete as he drew closer. His two giant nostrils sniffed as he came around the corner.

This was what I had been waiting for.

With a mighty cry to try and make myself feel braver than I was feeling, I launched myself on his snout, grabbing his horns. He shook his head, trying to throw me off, dashing his skull against the corner of the building like trying to wipe dog crap from a shoe.

But he was going to be smelling me for awhile longer. I took out my stake and nailed it right between his horns. He probably didn't even feel it, but that wasn't my intention. I had staked him just so I would have something to tie myself to. I straddled his head and fixed my stake to my utility belt. I was ready for this rodeo to begin.

He took off with a lurch. The entire world disappeared as he went straight up into the sky. It was like the worst motion simulator ride I had ever been on. I was completely ready to hurl. I gave him a kick in the eye to see if I could get him to behave himself.

He let out a roar and a stream of fire, but he headed back down to the ground.

That's when I saw Killian. He stood on the ground waving to the army he had rounded up. There were a good fifty gargoyles, some flying, some running, all looking like something charging the gates of Hell, which they were.

Killian pointed up at the bell tower and the gargoyles raced up the sides like monkeys up a tree. Really scary monkeys with big claws.

At first, I wasn't quite sure what they were up to, but then they showed me. They covered all sides of the bell. They shoved themselves up inside and around the clapper like frat boys in a phone booth. Killian looked up and suddenly I knew it was all up to me.

The dragon screamed forward, letting loose another wave of fire. It hit the bell, but the gargoyles hung on. The dragon put his head down and rammed it.

The bell flew out of the bell tower towards the ground.

"Hang on... hang on..." I muttered as I watched it, and all the gargoyles, go flying.

The bell split as it landed, but the ring was muffled.

Bell down.

It was done.

The bell was broken.

Sort of.

We still had this dragon on our hands. And I guess that's where I came in. I looped my rope over his horns and started scaling that dragon's scales like he was an REI wall and I was some sort of extreme rock climber. The dragon started doing barrel rolls, but I hung on. He stopped and changed directions. I felt my toes losing their grip. Then, suddenly, he stopped moving and just hovered in midair. I felt his limbs swiping at something. I looked up. The gargoyles were there, distracting him like gnats, flying at his eyes so he had to keep brushing them away. One of the gargoyles flew right by me and caught my foot just as it slipped, pushing me back into place. I dug my fingers deeper into the scales and kept going. There was his weak spot, right in the middle of his breastplate. I pulled my magical sword from its sheath and drove it home deep.

The dragon fell from the air with a cry, coating me with his hot blood.

I so had not signed up for this.

The dragon hit the ground and skidded. I leapt at the last moment, but was still tied to him. He dragged me across the parking lot, my leather coat and pants the only thing protecting me from the asphalt. As soon as he stopped twitching, I went over and pulled out my sword before the dragon's blood could coagulate on it. Then I summoned my courage, knowing what I had to do. I tried to remind myself that I eat hamburgers all the time and this was nothing more than what the local butcher at a grocery store has to put up with everyday.

I seriously started thinking about going vegan.

I plunged my arm into his thoracic cavity and pulled out his heartstone just as the dragon's body began to ignite.

I cut the rope and ran out of the way to safety, feeling victory swell within my soul. We had won!

And then out of nowhere, a werewolf ran by and knocked me down. The stone went tumbling out of my hand. His buddy came up fast behind him and grabbed it out of mid-air like dog catching a Frisbee.

I just lay there for a second, disbelieving.

I pulled out my gun and fired. Even though I hit them, they just kept on going like nothing happened. Vampwolves. Fucking vampwolves! Here! Stealing from ME! I watched them run out of the parking lot and down the street.

Did we just lose?

Did I really just slay two dragons in my lifetime to lose two heartstones? Were the dimensions about to collapse because of a fucking vampire-werewolf-mutt? Did we really get foiled at the last possible moment by Vaclav and his cronies?

I fired off a couple more rounds just because I was pissed. They were way too far away for me to hit them through the heart. I lowered my face to the ground and pressed my cheek against the blacktop of the playground.

Fuck.

We lost.

We fucking lost!

Killian plopped himself down beside me. He was covered with sweat and guts and blood. His perfect golden curly hair was dripping with grime, streaks ran down his filthy face. He stared off at where the vampwolves took off and didn't say a word. Then, he patted my back and said, "It will be all right, Maggie."

"How?" I asked. "How is this going to be all right?"

"We shall fix this."

"HOW?"

"I do not know," he replied. "But you always do, somehow. And so you shall with this. You always do."

That fucking elf just didn't know when we were beat. He just didn't know when to acknowledge that there was no way to win this. I was totally useless. Sure, the bell was gone and the dragon was dead, but we had a drafty window downstairs with a panoramic view of the Dark Dimension. It might not be big enough to let the big guys through, but as I looked at all the demons the gargoyles were bringing down from the sky, we were fucked. The most I could do right now was tear us open a hole to the Other Side so Killian could have a chance to say goodbye to his family.

His family...

I looked at his tights. At the bulge in his pants. Not THAT bulge. The other one. The one that might save us all.

"Killian!" I said, sitting up. I pushed back my hair. I couldn't believe I hadn't thought of it before. "Your family jewels!"

He looked at me strangely.

"Stop it! That ruby. That family ruby you were going to give to the dragon in exchange for the bell. Do you still have it?"

"Yes, I—" and then he got what I was getting at. He stood up, patting himself all over, not sure if he had it or not. But he did. He did. That elf could carry the goddamned world in his pockets!

He held up the ruby. It was what I thought it was. How could we have missed it all this time?

"It's a heartstone," I whispered.

He looked at me and nodded slowly. "Yes, Maggie. A stone that has been in my family for generations."

"A priceless gift which would have been valued by a dragon. AND the reason I couldn't feel a goddamned thing in the elfin forest!"

He reached out and grabbed my forearm, pulling me to my feet. I grabbed his hand, wrapping his fingers tight around the stone, holding his fist in mine. "Let's end this."

We ran. We ran like we had never run before. The sound of explosions were all around us. The sound of bodies slamming against the walls. There was death and destruction everywhere. We ran down into the catacomb. The roars of gargoyles and vampires and werewolves and every monster you could imagine echoed beneath the church. But we didn't stop. We turned the corner and there was the window.

It looked like an opening to a nuclear holocaust. The light was blindingly white, unleashing unholy hell all over this unhallowed spot. The cardinals were going to have a heck of a time getting this place reconsecrated.

Killian ripped his fireproof cloak off his shoulders and held it over the two of us like sweethearts in the rain. If it hadn't been for that cloak, we would have been melted like a slice of American cheese on a hot griddle.

"You're sure this is gonna hold, right?" I asked, shouting over the roar of the hellhole.

"It will hold," he yelled back.

"You sure?"

"Do not make me push you into the Dark Dimension, Maggie!"

There was a sound behind us and a creature of shadow and nightmares pulled itself from the darkest corner. This was not the little shadow who had tried to steal the bowl from us. This was his big bully brother and he was going to drag us somewhere we did not want to go.

Killian thrust the heartstone into my hand and dropped the cloak onto my shoulders. He pulled my sword from my side and squared off to face this shadow.

"You're going to get yourself killed!" I shouted.

"Go!" he yelled, pushing me forward. "Seal the hole!"

Killian stood behind me, using the protection of the cloak like a motorist drafting behind a semi-truck. The shadow tried to trick him to step out and into the storm.

I pushed forward, every step a victory. I reached up with the heartstone. The world slowed, all sound stopped, and in deafening silence, I placed the heartstone into the hole of the other stone.

And then the whole world exploded.

The window buckled beneath the weight of the Dark Dimension, it bent and wavered, but it held. The creature facing Killian fell to his knees. A wave of sound washed over all of us like a tsunami and then carried the dark creatures back like a riptide.

The heartstone sucked them in like water down a drain. There were screams and cries and roars.

And then it was done.

There was nothing but silence.

I felt the pieces of the boundary knitting themselves together. There would always be a weak spot here, a scar in the fabric of the universe, but it probably wasn't much worse than the hellhole the church had been holding closed anyways.

Killian and I both slid onto the floor of the mausoleum. The window darkened. There was a flash, then another flash, and then the light bulb behind it flickered, and popped, and then came on, illuminating its colored glass in a glorious wash of 60 watts.

I heard the sounds further down the hall of our good guys extracting themselves from the battlefield. A footstep here, the sound of rubble sliding there.

Exhausted, Killian reached out and patted my thigh. "See, Maggie? I told you. You always think of something."

"Sorry you had to give up your family heartstone," I said, too tired to even sit up.

He looked up at the window and the lovely red ruby in the middle. "I am glad to support Father Killarney's church. I believe this could be considered, according to my human studies professor, a 'tithe.'"

"A+, Killian. And I'm not even grading on a curve," I said.

"I think I preferred the church carnival."

Chapter 35

The day was won. The end was done. And I was looking forward to a holiday dinner at Mom and Dad's house. Dad had just driven Mindy and Austin in from Pasadena and was parking the car as Mindy waddled in. Killian gave a friendly wave with the silverware he was setting. I gave them a "Hello! My Darling" song and dance with the plates, using them like straw hats.

I heard the door slam and looked to see Dad take off his coat and gloves. Why the man needed gloves in the middle of the summer, I have no idea.

"Happy Solstice!" I said.

"Right back at you!" He pounded Killian on the back. "Glad you could join us!"

"Solstice is a time for reflection and family and gratitude. What better home to spend this holiday with?" He gave me a secret smile. I was going to have to find out what that was about. Can't have my partner going all mushy on me.

"Need help?" Dad asked as he grabbed a pickle off of the table.

Mom smacked his hands. "Don't spoil your dinner!"

"Sure!" I said to him, trying to avoid a family argument on this oh-so-special night. "Can you grab the bowls?"

Dad disappeared with Mom into the kitchen.

"You mean this bowl?" he shouted. He walked back in and pulled out that fucking meditation bowl which had started this whole damned thing from behind his back. "I fixed it!" And he gave it a sharp tap. The boundary crackled.

"WHAT THE FUCK!" I shouted.

"MAGGIE!" Mom yelled at me from the other room. "Watch that sort of language at the dinner table!"

"We aren't eating dinner yet!" I said as I lunged for the bowl. But Killian was two steps ahead of me. He grabbed it, ran into the TV room, tore the granny-square afghan from the back of the couch, and threw it over the bowl like it was on fire. He pummeled that thing into non-existence, muffling its tone in the pile of the shag carpet and crocheted love.

Breath heaving in his chest, he finally rose and held up the dented bowl. "I believe I have fixed it, too."

"Do you know how long it took me to figure out how to do that?!" my dad shouted.

"I hope it will take even longer for you to even consider recreating another one," Killian replied.

I looked over at Killian and we both broke into smiles, and then laughter.

That's what fucking partners are for.

"Ooo!" said Mindy, coming in with the salad and rubbing her belly. "The baby just kicked!"

Mom, Dad, and Austin crowded around her belly, cooing in amazement.

"MacKay babies do not kick, Mindy," said Killian, smiling at me through the hubbub. "They kick ass."

Yep, that's why you save the world.

Well, that's why I save it, anyway.

Find out what happens next to Maggie and Killian in
The M-Team!

And join the M-Team yourself by signing up for the
Kate Danley newsletter at maggieforhire.com

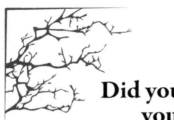

Did you like what you read?

- Sign up for the Kate Danley newsletter[1]
- Leave a nice review at your favorite online book re-tailer
- Tell your friends!
- Follow Kate on Facebook
- Visit www.katedanley.com to hear about upcoming releases and sales

Thank you!

Acknowledgements

This book was about new beginnings, a theme which has been reflected in my life. Because of your support, this year I became not just a full-time writer but a *USA TODAY* bestselling author. As I write this acknowledgement, there are over 200,000 copies of the *Maggie MacKay: Magical Tracker* series out in the wild and it has been optioned for film and television development. I cannot thank you enough. As an indie author, I don't have a massive marketing machine out there making my novels bestsellers. No publicist books me for radio shows and signings. I depend upon your word of mouth, your reviews, your kindness...YOU! You are my advertising. You are my marketing. You have made all this possible, and I cannot thank you enough.

If you like this series, please leave a kind review on your favorite online retailer. It is more important than you can even imagine. Please tell your friends. Just as my past was dependent upon your support for this success, so is my future. I would like to continue writing books for you, and promise I shall as fast as my fingers can fly.

Special thanks to my beta reader extraordinaire Adam Jackman! Thank you to all of my dear friends across the globe who have touched my life and kept me laughing: my Burbank gals, my blogger pals, my old friends, the OC/Phoenix/NYC contingencies, my Rose Bowl walkers, my writing buddies, my Shakespeare nerds, my Power Groups, my Towsonites, my producers and managers, my 47Northers, the good people I left behind at my day job, and all my sketch & improv & puppetry & film & theatre peeps. You form my brain in all its glory. But most of all, thank you to my family, who continually astounds me with their capacity for love and kindness and support. Fire up the BBC! I *will* be home for dinner!

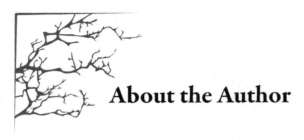

About the Author

U *SA TODAY* bestselling author Kate Danley is a twenty year veteran of stage and screen with 300+ credits to her name and a B.S. in theatre from Towson University. She was one of four students to be named a Maryland Distinguished Scholar in the Arts.

Her debut novel, *The Woodcutter* (published by 47North), was honored with the Garcia Award for the Best Fiction Book of the Year, the 1st Place Fantasy Book in the Reader Views Literary Awards, and the winner of the Sci-Fi/Fantasy category in the Next Generation Indie Book Awards.

Her plays have been produced in New York, Los Angeles, and Maryland. Her screenplay *Fairy Blood* won 1st Place in the Breckenridge Festival of Film Screenwriting Competition in the Action/Adventure Category and her screenplay American Privateer was a 2nd Round Choice in the Carl Sautter Memorial Screenwriting Competition.

Her projects *The Playhouse, Dog Days, Sock Zombie, Super-Pout*, and *Sports Scents* can be seen in festivals and on the internet. She trained in on-camera puppetry with Mr. Snuffleupagus and played the head of a 20-foot dinosaur on an NBC pilot.

She lost on Hollywood Squares.

The Maggie MacKay: Magical Tracker Series

http://www.maggiemackaymagicaltracker.com

LEGAL JUNK

This is a work of fiction. All of the characters, organizations, and events portrayed in this novel are either products of the author's imagination or are used fictitiously.

Made in the USA
Las Vegas, NV
10 February 2022